FIGHTING HAPPILY EVER AFTER

ELENA AITKEN

Also by Elena Aitken

Fighting For Forever

The Springs Collection: Volume 1

The Springs Collection: Volume 2

The Springs Collection: Volume 3

The Springs Complete Collection - Books 1-10

Timber Creek

When We Left

When We Were Us

When We Began

When We Fell

Castle Mountain Lodge

Unexpected Gifts

Hidden Gifts

Unexpected Endings - Short Story

Mistaken Gifts

Secret Gifts

Goodbye Gifts

Tempting Gifts

Holiday Gifts

Promised Gifts

Accidental Gifts

The Castle Mountain Lodge Collection: Books 1-3

The Castle Mountain Lodge Collection: Books 4-6

The Castle Mountain Lodge Collection: Books 7-9

The Castle Mountain Lodge Complete Collection

Halfway Series

Chapter One

THERE WAS SO much to do, and as was always the case, not enough time to get any of it done. Faith Turner downed the last of her cup of coffee and moved to refill it, but the pot was empty. *Empty.* She'd drank an entire pot of coffee. Bad coffee at that. She was definitely not known for her culinary skills, and somehow that extended to the simple act of making coffee.

Still, desperate times called for desperate measures and she was certainly desperate to stay awake. At least until she could cross some things off her to-do list. There was still a full month left in prime wedding season, and August was looking more and more like it would be a very full month for celebrations at Ever After Ranch, the wedding venue Faith now co-owned with her identical twin sister, Hope.

With Hope and her husband Levi on what was supposed to be a world-traveling honeymoon trip, the weddings had all fallen to Faith to plan *and* execute. A huge task for most, but especially for a woman who quite vocally and adamantly declared that the whole idea of love was bullshit. A wedding planner who didn't believe in love! Not even the most optimistic residents of Glacier Falls actually thought that Faith would be able to make a go of it. To be fair, neither did Faith herself.

Although, if she was asked—at least by a close friend—Faith might actually admit that her feelings on the matter were starting to change.

How could they not?

She'd witnessed more demonstrations of true love in the last few months at the ranch than she had in her entire life leading up to being a reluctant wedding planner. *Maybe there was something to it after all?*

The thought made her smile as she yanked the freshly washed sheets out of the dryer and headed up to the second floor of her childhood home. Her sister was coming home from her honeymoon much earlier than planned. Faith was not excited that the only reason Hope and Levi were coming home early was because of Hope's health. But still, it would be good to have her home. Especially considering she was pregnant.

Never mind the cancer diagnosis that Hope had received right before quickly getting married and jetting off on an around-the-world adventure, where she got knocked up.

No matter what the circumstances, it would be good to have her close again. Their arrival was still a few days away, but if she didn't get their room made up now, it wouldn't happen. The next few days were going to be packed. There'd be little time for making beds, let alone sleeping. With one last wistful thought toward her empty coffee pot, Faith made quick work of the bed and headed back to her own room, stripping her clothes off and scattering them on the floor as she went.

She wasn't a messy person as a general rule, and her lowered standards were going to have to be picked up again soon with Hope and Levi moving in, but at least for a few more days she'd have the place to herself.

Faith let the hot shower water steam up in her attached bathroom before stepping inside and closing the glass door behind her. It felt good to let the water melt the tension from her shoulder muscles and she dropped her head back into the stream with a satisfied sigh.

She had a huge meeting later this morning with probably the biggest client Ever After Ranch had ever seen. Stephanie Starz was the hottest celebrity in Hollywood and if she wanted to get married at the ranch, well, Faith was going to make sure she pulled it off and give Stephanie the wedding of her dreams. Despite the minor detail that she was deeply in over her head.

She should be preparing. Going over her notes one last time about the latest movies Stephanie had been in and the little Canadian town she herself had grown up in so Faith could relate it to Glacier Falls and why it was the perfect place for her to get married. In fact, she probably didn't have time to really enjoy the shower or dillydally at all. But the hot water felt so good that she allowed herself the luxury of a few more minutes before working the shampoo into her long blonde locks.

She closed her eyes and once more tipped her head back, letting the hot water soothe her. A groan escaped her lips as the sudsy water washed out and down the drain. *How was it that a simple shower could feel so damn good?*

"I wish my showers were so satisfying."

What the—

Faith's head shot up, but with soap in her eyes, she wiped at them, trying to see the owner of the voice. Not that she needed to. She knew exactly who had just walked into her *bathroom!*

"What the fuck, Logan?" Faith screamed and tried in vain to cover her body. Although the steamy glass door was probably providing some privacy. "I'm in the *shower!*"

"Oh, don't worry," came his reply. "I can see that."

She didn't have to see his eyes to know how they would have gleamed with the comment. And that little detail alone was enough to infuriate her. She shouldn't know him so well. *But she did.*

And it pissed her off almost more than the fact that he was in her bathroom uninvited.

"Get out!" she hissed.

"No can do, Faith."

"What?" She was going to start throwing shampoo bottles at him if he didn't get his ass out of her bathroom—and soon. "Of course you can."

"Well, sure. I can…but I'm moving in, so I need to—"

"You are *what?*"

Logan was a lot of things. Primarily, he was way too cocky for his own good, way too sexy for *her* own good, and besides both of those things, an almost constant, annoying presence in her life. Like a pebble in her shoe. Yes, he was a lot of things. But an idiot wasn't one of them. So why would he think he was—

"Oh no," she said as soon as she connected the dots in her head. "You are *not* moving in."

"I have to," he said simply. "You're the love of my life, remember?"

———

Logan Langdon was very aware that he was pushing it. A lot. He was also very aware that he was enjoying every moment of it. Faith Turner was sexy, sassy, and—whether she would ever admit it or not—completely into him.

But damn, he certainly hoped she'd admit it—and soon. Because as much fun as it was to pursue her, he was positively certain that it would be even more fun to *catch* her.

"You are not the love of my life, Logan." Faith's voice started to reach an impressively high frequency. "Get. Out. Of. My. *Bathroom!*"

Leaving her alone was probably for the best. After all, she *was* in the shower. It hadn't been his intention to interrupt her privacy, but he couldn't lie. Now that he, too, was in the bathroom with her naked, wet body only a few feet away, it was the last place he wanted to leave.

Still.

Logan grabbed a large towel off a nearby hook and draped it over the edge of the glass. "Here. Cover up if you must. But I'm not leaving. I'm moving in." He grinned even though he knew she wouldn't see it, turned and left the bathroom to wait for her in the adjoining bedroom.

Logan didn't miss the growl of frustration she let out as he left the room, nor did he miss the tightening in his belly at the sound. There was something about riling her up that he enjoyed. Maybe a little too much.

He didn't have to wait long for a dripping wet, steaming mad Faith, wrapped in only the towel he'd provided her, to join him.

Fuck. Should have given her a smaller towel.

The image made his lips curl up into a grin.

"What are you smiling at?" she demanded. "And what the hell are you doing here?"

Even if he hadn't put the picture of Faith in a much smaller towel in his head, Logan would have been distracted. After all, the most gorgeous woman he knew, with all of her perfectly proportioned curves, currently stood directly in front of him. The soft mounds of her breasts pushed up from where she'd cinched the towel around her. The opening of said towel displayed just enough thigh for him to fixate on, with her long blonde hair hanging wet over her shoulders, giving an air of some watery fantasy vibes that, more than anything, Logan desperately wanted to explore.

He swallowed hard and hoped his arousal wasn't betraying him too obviously because it was taking all the self-control he had not to pull her in for a kiss to show her exactly what it was that she did to him. If that last kiss they'd shared was any indication, he was sure that those feelings weren't completely one-sided. Not that she was going to admit it.

Not yet, anyway.

"Logan! Are you even listening to me?"

Yanked from his fantasies of what was under the towel, Logan refocused on the issue at hand. He was moving in and she was clearly not happy about it.

He swallowed hard and turned to the dresser, pulling open a drawer. "I was just wondering which drawers I could make mine." He grinned as he reached inside and pulled out a silky pair of light-pink panties. "Pink, huh? I didn't take you for a baby-pink kind of woman." He dangled the panties in front of him. "Red? Definitely. Black? Absolutely. But soft pink?" He pressed his lips together in an effort not to smirk. "Now that is a surprise."

Faith's face had also turned a specific shade of pink. But there was nothing soft about it when she reached out and yanked her panties from his grip before reaching past him and the drawer shut so violently he almost got his hand caught inside.

"Get. Out. Logan."

Okay. He was definitely pushing her too far.

He let his eyes drop to where her towel had slipped a little and for a split second contemplated again how it might turn out if he just gave in and kissed her. But the anger flashing in her eyes told him it wouldn't be a good idea.

"Okay," he finally conceded. "I'll let you get dressed and then we can talk." He watched her visibly—at least a little—relax as he spoke. "Because we do need to talk about this, Faith, and you know it." She nodded but she still didn't look pleased. "Don't forget, you're the love of my life." Her lips pressed together in a hard line when he added, "At least for the next few weeks."

By the time Faith managed to pull on a T-shirt and cutoff shorts and pull her still soaking hair up into a clip, she'd managed to calm down a little. But only a little. She was still vibrating—and mostly with anger, although she couldn't deny the flip of her stomach or the clenching of her gut whenever Logan was around. Never mind the fact that she was naked in the shower and he was in her underwear drawer.

Ugh.

Okay. She was still pretty mad. And she'd need to focus on that anger to keep her from letting any of the other feelings through. Especially because the alternative was to admit that the man's mere presence did things to her insides that made her want to drop her towel completely. No matter how mad she was.

Faith took a deep breath and let it out slowly before walking into the kitchen, where Logan was pouring two cups of freshly brewed coffee. He handed her one when she walked in and despite herself, she inhaled the delicious aroma deeply. He made a damned good cup of coffee and she was sorely in need of it.

"Are you ready to talk about me moving in now?" he said after she'd sat at the kitchen table.

"It's not happening."

"Faith. It has to." He sat down across from her. "You do remember what's happening today, right? The meeting? *The* meeting."

She remembered. She also remembered very clearly what lie they'd perpetuated to get that meeting. It didn't matter that they hadn't actually started the lie, but they'd definitely run with it.

"Remember," Logan said. "It's not our fault that Stephanie Starz thinks we're madly in love. We never told her that."

"Not yet."

Logan didn't respond and they both knew it was because it would only be a matter of hours before they did, in fact, lie to Hollywood's biggest celebrity and tell her that they were in love and they'd found that love right there on Ever After Ranch. Just the way her twin sister and Levi had before them. And just the way the online wedding site, *Weddings Weekly*, had reported it. Complete with a picture of Faith and Logan in what could only be described as a very passionate kiss.

Because it had been.

The truth of the matter was that the photographer, who'd taken the picture during a professional photo shoot she'd hired him for, hadn't mentioned at all that Logan had only been trying to *demonstrate* how a couple in love should kiss to their friends Sarah and Brody, who were the models of the shoot who happened to be in the middle of a giant argument at the time and were having trouble playing make-believe. No. None of the actual details had been mentioned. Only a completely fabricated story about how Ever After Ranch was the most romantic wedding venue around and how could it not be when both of the identical twin sister owners had found their very own happily ever after right there?

Faith had to admit, it had been brilliant free marketing. Even if it was based on a lie. And it never would have resulted in anything more if Stephanie Starz hadn't contacted her to request a personal visit to the ranch to consider it for her very own, very much publicized nuptials.

"It's an innocent little lie," Logan said. "It's not going to hurt anyone and, if anything, it will benefit everyone. The entire town of Glacier Falls will benefit from this wedding. It's the biggest wedding of the—"

"Century," she finished for him. "I know. But it's still…"

"Don't tell me you're backing out of the bet?"

His eyes flashed with mischief because damn him, he knew she wasn't going to back out of the bet. Which was exactly why she never should have agreed to it in the first place. Because *she* knew better.

Still. When Logan had bet her that she didn't have it in her to act like a loved-up couple with him long enough to pull off the wedding of the century, she'd had no other choice but to accept it. Despite the terms. If she won, he'd back off on pursuing her and driving her crazy. And if he won…something about spending an entire night with him. She was trying not to think about that. For a variety of reasons.

The terms of the bet were suspect at best. Still, she hadn't been able to say no. She never could when it came to Logan. Ever since they were in high school, he had an uncanny ability to drive her crazy and push all her buttons.

"Of course I'm not backing out." She took a sip of her coffee and tried not to moan. *Damn it. It was really good.*

"Good." He wiggled his eyebrows. "Because I'm looking forward to winning."

Faith shook her head and rolled her eyes. There was no point getting into it with him. Instead, she switched tacks. "About you moving in. It's not—"

"Oh, it's happening, Faith, and you know it." Logan's face lost its cocky grin and turned serious in a flash. "This has to look convincing. If Stephanie suspects that our love isn't legit, she might pull the whole idea of having her wedding at Ever After before we even get the gig. And you know as well as I do that having this here will be huge." He shook his head. "Bigger than huge. It will be—"

"Massive," she agreed reluctantly. As much as she hated to

admit it, Logan was right. And with Hope and Levi on their way home so Hope could stay on bed rest, the publicity from this event would be exactly what they needed to take build the business at Ever After Ranch. It was way beyond what Faith had been planning when she started to dream up a social media marketing campaign. This was next level. And it was important.

"Okay," she said after a moment. "But you're not staying in my room with me."

"Where else am I going to sleep?"

"We have a spare bedroom." Faith made a mental note to find a minute to clear out the boxes and things that had been stored in their spare room for who knows how long, but before she could say more about it, Logan was shaking his head.

"No can do. That's going to be the baby's room, and Levi already texted me about helping him out with getting it ready for Hope as a surprise."

Levi and Logan were cousins and ever since Levi's mother had died when he was younger, he'd been raised with Logan and his little sister on their ranch down the road. They were more like brothers than cousins, and it was no surprise that Logan would be called into duty to help Levi out. What was a surprise was this entire situation. And more and more, it looked as if Faith wasn't going to win this particular argument.

She hated not winning the argument. Especially against Logan.

She took another sip of coffee and let the rich aroma fill her senses before putting her mug down and looking Logan in the eye. "Fine," she said slowly. "But fresh coffee every morning when I wake up is part of the deal."

"Of course." A slow, sexy smile crossed his face. "Now you better go get ready because we have a celebrity to impress."

Chapter Two

LOGAN HAD NEVER CONSIDERED himself the type of guy who would ever be star struck. After all, celebrities were just regular people who happen to be famous. So he was in no way prepared for Stephanie Starz and the energy she projected the second she stepped out of her rented luxury SUV. She was shorter than she appeared on the screen, a petite, fiery, incredibly gorgeous redhead who, judging by the first few minutes of meeting her, was also a genuinely nice person. Her smile and bubbly personality made him instantly warm to her.

He could see that Faith was equally affected by the woman, who despite being the world's biggest superstar, had arrived alone. Without any assistants, bodyguards, or any entourage at all, proclaiming that she was hoping to keep her visit as low-key and under the radar as possible.

Logan had no idea how they were going to accomplish that particular feat, considering that even if she wasn't incredibly famous and recognizable, she was also absolutely gorgeous, and he knew of at least a few single men in town who would be tripping all over themselves just to say hello, celebrity or not.

But not him.

As stunning as Stephanie was, she had nothing on Faith. Petite redheads weren't his type. But tall, curvy blondes? Now that was exactly the type of woman who got his heart racing. Especially when he had one arm wrapped around her, with his hand resting in what he hoped came off as a casual way on said blonde's waist. He was more than happy to use every opportunity to touch Faith and hold her close. Especially considering he knew that because of the situation they were in she couldn't react the way she had their entire life and push him away.

"So?" Faith asked Stephanie after they'd done a mini tour of the ranch. "Obviously we have so much more to show you, but what are your first impressions?"

Stephanie pressed her lips together and nodded to herself for a moment.

Next to him, Logan could feel Faith tense. He reached out and grabbed her hand. They both wanted Stephanie to love the ranch enough to hold her wedding there, of course. But although Faith wanted it for the benefit of the ranch and the business, his reasons were purely selfish. The wedding at Ever After would mean that he got to keep pretending to be the love of Faith's life and maybe if they pretended enough, he might actually be able to convince her that he wasn't, and had never had been, pretending.

Logan held his breath, but he didn't have to wait long for Stephanie's answer.

"Oh my God," she gushed a moment later. Her hands clasped together, the giant diamond on her left hand flashing in the sunlight. "Your ranch is…" She waved her hands around dramatically, in what could only be described as a windmill action. "Perfect!" she finished. "It's absolutely perfect! I don't know if you know this, but I grew up in a small town in Northern Canada and I love the idea of coming *home* for such a special day. And not only is your ranch absolutely beautiful…" She turned to face them. "It's *so* lucky," she effused. "I mean, what are the odds that identical twins have *both* found their true loves right here at their very own wedding venue? It's magical, is what it is, and I would be honored to be part of that magic, even in some small way."

Faith pulled away from Logan and opened her arms to Stephanie, whom, up until about forty minutes earlier, had been a complete stranger. Not that it mattered. As was often the case when it came to women, Logan was left shaking his head when Stephanie Starz readily accepted the hug and the two embraced like long-lost friends.

He couldn't help but grin because clearly, even without a contract signed, it looked as if Ever After would be hosting the wedding of the century between Stephanie Starz and Dax Combs, which meant he got to stay cuddled up with Faith a little bit longer.

"This is fantastic news." He clapped his hands together. "Ever After is the perfect place for love, and I'm not just saying that because I'm biased." Logan stepped forward and Stephanie welcomed him into an embrace as well.

"You two really are the sweetest couple," she said. "I mean, obviously I was completely blown away by the article online when I saw the two of you together. That kind of chemistry is just so…" She waved her hands in the air. It was becoming very clear that Stephanie was a very passionate hand talker. "Powerful," she finished. "You two are just so clearly in love with each other and for that to be so clearly depicted in a photo? I have to tell you how rare that is. And, if I'm being totally honest, I half expected to be disappointed when I met you both. I mean, you can't possibly be that much in love, right?" She laughed.

Next to him, Faith giggled nervously, but he kept smiling.

"But you are!" Stephanie continued. "And I absolutely

cannot wait to meet your sister and her new husband. You said they were coming home soon?"

"Yes. In two days, actually. It's really too bad that they aren't here for you to—"

"Oh good." Stephanie cut her off. "Do you think I'll get a chance to see them, too?"

"Well, I'm not sure how long you're staying in town," Faith said with a smile. "But I'm sure we can arrange something if the timing works out."

Stephanie dipped her head for a moment before looking up again. "I know this is going to sound crazy."

Logan highly doubted that there could possibly be any more crazy in this particular situation, but he didn't say so.

"But now that I'm here, I kind of don't want to leave."

Faith chuckled a little. "Glacier Falls does have that effect on people, but I don't understand. I was under the impression that you'd be here for a few days so we could show you around a bit more."

"Oh yes," Stephanie said quickly. "But now I'm thinking… well…you can tell me if this is crazy or not okay with you in any way, but I'd really like to stay for a bit longer than that. Just to get a feel for the place, you know? And be as involved as possible with you and planning the wedding. All the details, everything."

"Everything?"

Logan looked between the two women with a grin on his face. They'd always planned on having the celeb around for a few days—that's why he was able to convince Faith to let him move in—but for some indeterminate amount of time? That would change things—in all the right ways. And he couldn't think of a better situation if it meant he got to get even closer to Faith for weeks, rather than just days. Faith, on the other hand…she didn't look quite as pleased.

Logan watched while she clearly tried to think of an excuse that would be acceptable to her biggest client ever.

Coming up with nothing, she swallowed hard and smiled. "That would be fantastic."

It was a bald-faced lie, but no one besides Logan knew it.

"The summer? The *whole* summer?"

Stephanie Starz had left only ten minutes earlier, leaving Faith and Logan alone in the barn where they held the receptions for their weddings. They were supposed to be getting set up for the upcoming event in a few days, but Faith couldn't concentrate. Not when her newest, and biggest, client had just dropped a major bomb on her.

What the hell was she going to do with Hollywood's biggest celebrity hanging around for the entire summer? Okay, maybe it wasn't the *whole* summer, but a few weeks in August. Might as well be. It wasn't that she didn't like Stephanie; she did. In fact, she'd been pleasantly surprised at how much she'd liked the woman. Not that Faith really knew what to expect considering she'd never met a famous person even close to the same level as Stephanie Starz. But whatever she'd been thinking, it definitely wasn't that the petite redhead would be a genuinely nice person. Someone she would actually enjoy spending time with.

Which was good, because it looked as if they were going to spend a whole lot of it together.

"I think it will be good." Logan wiggled his eyebrows. "And frankly, I think it's going to be a whole lot of fun."

"Fun?"

"Of course." He put down the chair he was moving, rested his hands on the back of it, and looked at her. "It's going to be a ton of fun to be madly in love with you for the rest of the summer."

Her stomach clenched and she had to look away lest her face betray whatever it was that was going on inside her. Because for the life of her, Faith could not figure out why she was having such strong reactions to Logan. Reactions that got stronger and stronger every time they were together. He'd always been able to get under her skin. Ever since they were teenagers, he could rile her up. But this was different. These *feelings* were different. These involved full-body reactions that made her want to—well, they made her want to do a lot of things that were probably a very bad idea.

"It's only for a few weeks," Faith said. "Stephanie's wedding will be...well...whenever it is... and then...and then we can stage some sort of *breakup* and forget this ever happened."

Logan pretended to be hurt. His hand fluttered to his chest and his mouth fell open, miming shock. "Faith Turner, you don't mean that."

She crossed her arms and nodded. "You know I do." She glared at him until he turned and walked away to get more chairs. As soon as his back was turned, she dropped her head to her chest and let out a long breath. It was going to be a very long month if every time he looked at her, it caused her stomach to do a summersault as if she were some giggly pre-teen with a crush. She took a deep breath and then another.

Get a hold of yourself. You're stronger than this.

And she was. She had self-declared from a very young age that she wanted nothing to do with a relationship. Ever. She'd spent her entire adult life perfecting the art of getting close enough to have a good time, but not too close to actually feel anything. And it had worked, too. There'd been a few close calls when she'd maybe started to care a little too much, but she'd always been able to stop her feelings before they went too far.

This was different, though.

Logan was different.

Her feelings—or whatever they were—were different. In the last few months since she'd been back in Glacier Falls, planning and executing the weddings at Ever After, with Logan helping every step of the way—mostly as a favor to her sister and his cousin—she'd started to experience what could only be described as a change of heart. Watching some of her closest and oldest friends fall in love, or recognize the love they'd always had and had been hiding from, changed a person. Even a person as dead set against the whole *love* thing as Faith was. She'd actually started considering the fact that she'd been wrong for all those years and maybe she *had* been missing out after all.

And maybe…just maybe…Logan had a little something to do with that.

Faith sighed.

Or, more likely, Logan was just doing what Logan did best and working her up because he could. He'd always made it his special mission to piss her off, push her buttons, and get a reaction out of her. This situation was no different.

She shook her head clear. They had work to do. "Logan," she called out as she turned around. "Can you grab me three more—"

Her words dissolved on her tongue, as Logan's strong arms wrapped around her and pulled her in hard against his chest. Taller than her, he looked down into her eyes, and tipped her chin up with a finger and a thumb before kissing the question right off her lips. To her horror, her knees buckled a little and electricity buzzed through her, lighting up even the darkest parts of her. It didn't last long, but it didn't have to. When he pulled away, her fingers moved to her lips and she shook her head slightly.

"What the hell, Logan?"

He shrugged. "I thought I heard a vehicle pull up. I

17

thought maybe if it was Stephanie, that would really sell it. But..." He shrugged again. "I guess I was wrong."

Faith didn't miss the twinkle in his eye, and a steel resolve replaced the warmth he'd just infused her body with. He was definitely taking the piss because he thought he could get away with it.

"Logan!"

He turned around again, a small smile on his lips. No doubt he thought her anger was amusing.

"That's not okay," she continued, trying to control her voice. "You can't just—"

Once more his lips were on hers. His hand was behind her head, holding her to him as his mouth worked against hers. Her body betrayed her as she instinctively kissed him back and pressed into it.

Behind her somewhere she vaguely registered the creak of the barn door and the unmistakable sound of boots on the hardwood. Maybe he hadn't been taking the piss; maybe he was simply putting on a show for Stephanie.

"Oh. I didn't mean to interrupt."

But it wasn't their new celebrity client. But a recognizable voice nonetheless.

Faith pulled back from Logan, pushing him in the chest a little as she stepped away and turned to greet Brody Morris, their friend who also happened to own Birchwood, the best restaurant in town, as well as Ever After Ranch's exclusive caterer. "You weren't interrupting," she said while trying to wipe her lips as discreetly as she could. "Logan was just..."

"Trying to show me how it was done again?" Brody laughed and Logan joined in.

If she hadn't been so startled by everything, Faith might have joined in as well, especially because it was Brody and his new fiancée Sarah whom Logan had been *demonstrating* the kiss for in the photo shoot that had changed everything and brought them their biggest client yet.

"You know it, buddy." Logan smacked Brody on the back as they laughed together while Faith rolled her eyes.

They hadn't decided on whether they should tell their friends the truth about their *just for show* relationship or not, so for the time being, Faith opted just to keep her mouth shut and try to change the subject. "I assume you're here to talk about this weekend's menu. Why don't we go into the kitchen and work out the details? Logan can finish up out here, can't you, Logan?"

"You know I can, babe."

Babe?

She shot him a look while Brody chuckled, but Logan only winked and blew her a kiss.

It was going to be a very long summer.

Chapter Three

LOGAN FINISHED PUTTING the tools back in the shed and closed it up. He'd been spending less and less time on the Langdon ranch all summer. Ever since taking on the task of helping Faith out with Ever After, there hadn't been time for both. Thankfully, his mother had hired a few ranch hands who were more than capable of looking after things. For the most part, anyway. Even so, Logan liked to pop in and make sure everything was under control. He knew he was shirking his duties as a son, especially considering his father had passed away earlier that year. He was no stranger to the guilt that filled him every time he drove away from his family ranch and toward Faith. But like a magnet pull, he couldn't seem to stop himself.

He found his mother, Debbie, in the kitchen, putting the finishing touches on a roast dinner that she was laying on the table for the two of them. "Mom," Logan said from the sink where he washed up. "You didn't have to go to so much trouble just for me. I would have been happy with a grilled cheese sandwich and tomato soup."

She flicked a dishtowel in his direction and shook her head.

"I like cooking for you, and I don't get the chance very often these days, so let me do it. Besides, you can take leftovers back to Faith's house with you." Her smile dipped a little. "I was hoping you'd bring her tonight," she added. "It's been awhile since I've seen her, too."

He shrugged. He hadn't even asked Faith to come for dinner. Mostly because he was certain she would say no, but also because he knew she had plans with the girls to go to Birchwood for dinner. "I told you, we aren't a couple," he said instead. "Not really. We're just—"

"I know, I know. You're just pretending."

Debbie put a basket of rolls on the kitchen table and gestured for her son to sit down before pulling out the chair across from him, where she'd sat every night of his life. Despite the fact that she was now a widow with two grown children and almost singlehandedly in charge of an entire ranch on her own, she still looked youthful, with only a few little wrinkles around her eyes defying her true age. Logan couldn't help but wonder if she'd ever date again. After all, she was so young to be widowed, with a whole life ahead of her still, if she decided to. As much as he'd loved his father, and he knew his mother had too, he really did hope that one day she'd be able to move on and find happiness again with someone else.

"I don't know what it is about my children." Debbie speared a slab of roast off the platter. "What did I do wrong, raising you both to think it's okay to fake a relationship? And not one, but both of you now."

"Katie and Damon were different." He accepted the bowl of potatoes from her, scooping out a healthy portion. Earlier that summer, his little sister Katie had pretended to be engaged and then very quickly thereafter, married to her billionaire best friend, without anyone knowing. Of course, the two of them had always been in love but hadn't bothered admitting it to themselves, let alone each other, and as soon as they figured out that one very important detail, they got married *for real* and were now happier than Logan had ever seen either of them.

The thing with Faith was different.

"I don't see how it's any different," Debbie said. "You're lying about your relationship."

He shrugged. "But I told *you* the truth. And don't forget you can't tell anyone. I mean…some people will probably figure it out, but…" He gave her a goofy grin, but she shot him a look. "Besides, Katie and Damon were totally in love with each other. It was ridiculous and obvious."

"And that's different from you and Faith, how?"

Logan froze, a piece of beef halfway to his mouth. *How was it different?* Well, for one thing, they weren't in love. Sure, Logan always had a thing for Faith; that wasn't a secret. *But love?* That was a bit farfetched. Particularly considering his mere presence seemed to piss Faith off more and more every day. *No. It was different. Very different.*

"Oh, it's different," he finally said as he stuffed the meat into his mouth. "And it's only to land this big wedding, which is even more important now, because Levi and Hope are coming home."

That got her attention the way he knew it would. "They're coming home? When? Is everything okay?" Levi had always been like another son to Debbie, and she'd been ecstatic at the news that they were expecting. "Why didn't he call me?"

"I told him I'd let you know. It's all been a little rushed with everything."

"Is Hope okay?" Her face shifted at once into worry and stress. "The baby? Is the baby—"

"The baby's fine and Hope's fine." His mother visibly calmed at the news, but rolled her eyes as he continued. "But she does have high blood pressure, I think Faith said. Or something like that, so they—"

"How come men never pay attention to the details?"

He shrugged and scooped up some more potatoes. "This is delicious, Mom. I really am going to miss this cooking, living at Faith's. She can't even brew coffee."

"And why was it that you *needed* to move in there again?"

Logan did his best to ignore the way his mom wiggled her eyebrows. *Why was it that moms thought they knew everything?*

"Because we need it to look real. And Stephanie is staying in town for a while."

"Stephanie?" She tilted her head. "So you're on a first-name basis with this celebrity now, are you?"

Logan shrugged. She'd seemed far more down-to-earth than he'd expected her to be and without the entourage he'd expected, too. She really was just a normal person trying to find a nice location for her wedding. If anything, she seemed a bit lonely. And he told his mom so.

"Well, I'm sure you'll have a lot of fun with Faith showing this *Stephanie* around town."

Logan shook his head and speared a carrot with his fork.

"Not that I think spending all that time with Faith will be much of a hardship for you." She winked and Logan could no longer ignore whatever it was she was insinuating.

"Mom." He put his fork down and clasped his hands together over his plate. "I told you. It's not like that. This whole thing is different than it was with Damon and Katie. We're just—"

"Oh, I know what you're doing," she interrupted him. "And you may think it's different, but—"

"It *is*, Mom."

"Okay." She held her hands up in a mock surrender and smiled sweetly. "If you say so, dear."

"I needed this. Thank you for joining me tonight." Faith lifted her glass of wine in a quick toast to her girlfriends gathered around the table at Birchwood before taking a deep swallow of the crisp, cool liquid. "It's been a crazy week."

"And it's only just begun," Sarah Lewis added as she, too, drank from her glass. "I heard it's been a little...well, what's the word..."

"Busy," Faith supplied for her. "It's been *busy*." There was no doubt that Sarah's fiancé, Brody, who'd walked in on Logan kissing her the day before, had filled her in on all the details. And Faith wouldn't be surprised if Nicole, Sarah's sister-in-law, sitting next to her, also knew the details. Especially considering Nicole's new wife, Amy, was Brody's head chef.

There were times when Faith had to seriously question her decision in moving back to such a small town where everyone knew everyone and were just as involved in their personal lives.

"I didn't hear how *busy* things have been." Across from her, Katie Banks, Logan's little sister, raised an eyebrow. "But it sounds super juicy."

Faith shook her head. The last thing she wanted to talk about with Katie was her big brother, and they were definitely going to need another bottle. "There's nothing juicy about being busy."

"Not unless it involves a certain celebrity," Katie persisted.

"Oh!" Faith paused, her glass halfway to her mouth. "You were talking about Stephanie Starz juicy."

Katie gave her a look. "What did you think I was talking about?"

"Nothing." Faith quickly took another drink of her wine and picked up her menu. "We should order." Her eyes lifted a little and locked directly on Sarah, who was watching her with a very knowing expression on her face.

Dammit. Brody had definitely filled her in on the kiss he'd caught them in.

A kiss that still sent thrills through her, despite the fact that she had every reason not to feel anything for Logan or his kisses.

Faith quickly looked away, but when Sarah cleared her voice—loudly—she turned back to her friend. "Yes?"

"I was just wondering if you were planning on filling us in on the rest of your *business*?"

All eyes turned to Faith. They hadn't really decided on what to tell their friends about their *relationship* as it was so publicly announced, and for the most part, there hadn't been a need to say anything at all because most people just assumed the article that had appeared on *Weddings Weekly* was a hilarious misunderstanding—which it was—and hadn't bothered to push the issue. But now...

Faith sighed.

On one hand, she hated to lie to her friends. But, on the other hand, if one of them blew their cover with Stephanie Starz, it would all be for naught. Besides, Logan *had* bet her she couldn't do it. And she hated to back down from a bet. Especially one from Logan. She took a deep breath and gave her friends what they were looking for.

"Oh," she said as casually as she could manage. "You must be talking about the fact that Logan and I are——"

"You're together, aren't you?" Katie all but jumped out of her chair with excitement. "I knew it. I knew that article wasn't bullshit. I just knew it."

Faith worked hard not to roll her eyes. Katie didn't know anything, not really, but there was nothing to be gained by pointing it out. Particularly considering she'd just made the lying portion of things so much easier.

"I was waiting for you to say something," Sarah jumped in. "But Brody did mention that he walked in on what looked like a pretty private moment yesterday."

"I wouldn't say it was private..."

"Okay," Sarah amended. "He said it was *intense*. I believe his exact words were *an intense kiss*."

"I wouldn't say it was intense…"

"If it was anything like the kiss in that picture online, it was definitely intense." It was Nicole's turn to jump in. "Personally, I've always thought the two of you had an intensity together."

Intensity? What was with the word choice?

Faith reached for her glass, but realized it was empty and tried not to sigh out loud. "Anyway," she said. "It's really not a big deal, but we are——"

"Not a big deal?" Katie was still bouncing in her seat. "You're going to be my sister-in-law. I'd say that's a pretty big deal."

"Whoa." Faith grabbed the bottle and poured what was left, which was very little, into her glass before downing that, too. "No one is saying anything about getting married. We're just…" *What? What were they?* "We're just taking it slow." *There. That's what people said.* "We don't want to rush anything."

Katie settled back into her seat and the rest of her friends looked placated for the time being. But if Faith knew anything about this particular group of friends, it was that they weren't going to stay that way for long. And no doubt by the time dinner was done, word would have spread even further around town until everyone knew that she was *with* Logan.

"We should order more wine." Faith waved the now empty bottle over the table.

"And food," Nicole said. "Amy's in charge of the kitchen tonight, and she insisted on making us a special meal if we wanted it." Nicole quickly glanced over at Sarah. "I think she cleared it with Brody first."

"I'm looking forward to it." Sarah laughed. "I love Brody's cooking, but I think I've had everything on the menu already. It's too bad Amy can't be out here with us, but I suppose if Brody's out with the guys, someone has to be in charge."

"Out with the guys?" Faith tore her attention from the wine list. If Brody was out *with the guys* that meant Logan was too, which meant they better have their stories straight.

"Yup," Sarah said. "Something about meeting up with Logan, Damon, Jeremy, and Damon's friend Nick at the Knot. I have to say, we're definitely getting the better food."

Everyone laughed because their local watering hole, the Knot, was a lot of fun and served great drinks, but it was absolutely not known for its cuisine.

Faith pushed out of her chair. "Can you order another bottle of whatever it was we just had?" she said to Sarah. "And I'm happy to have whatever delicious creation Amy comes up with. I just have to make a quick phone call. Sorry. I'll be right back."

———

Logan had just sat down with the guys and ordered a beer when his cell phone rang. His first instinct was to ignore it. After all, whatever it was could wait until he'd had at least one sip of the cold draft that was about to be delivered. He made the mistake of glancing at the screen. A photo of Faith, taken at the beach when they had gone as a large group the month before, filled the screen. She was smiling. Sun-kissed and totally relaxed, she was completely irresistible. He had to answer it.

"I'll be right back," he told the guys and excused himself outside to take the call.

"Hey," he said as soon as he stepped out the heavy wooden doors. "What's up?"

"Did you tell them?"

Logan couldn't help but grin. "Tell them what exactly? And furthermore, who is *them*?"

"Did you tell the guys that we're together?" She was clearly trying not to raise her voice and her face was probably that cute shade of pink that it always got when she got worked up.

"Was I supposed to?"

"Logan!"

He knew he was only making her stress more, but he couldn't help it. Getting Faith riled up was a deeply ingrained reflex. "I didn't tell them anything," he said after a moment. "But mostly because I didn't get the chance yet. I just sat down. I don't even have a beer yet." His thoughts drifted to the cold drink that was probably being delivered to the table as they spoke. There was nothing quite like a cold beer on a hot summer night.

"They know," Faith said, ignoring the mention of his absent beverage. "They already know. Brody saw us kissing and of course he told Sarah, which means that Amy and Nicole know, and I'm not sure about Damon and Katie and what they knew or didn't know, but I more or less had to admit that we were together, and now I'm pretty sure that your sister is planning our wedding. It's all—"

"Calm down." He couldn't help the smile that crossed his face at the idea of all their friends being excited for them that they were a couple. Despite the fact that it was a lie—at least for now—it still spoke to the fact that they liked the idea of them together. "Wasn't that the idea?" he asked. "Everyone is supposed to think it's real, right? At least for a little bit. They'll understand. Everyone understood when Katie and Damon faked their relationship."

"It's not the same."

No. It wasn't the same. Despite what his mother said.

"Are you getting cold feet?" he teased. "Maybe you can't hack it. Pretending to be with me? I knew you wouldn't last—"

"I'm not getting cold feet." Her voice had lost any edge of panic. "And I can absolutely hack it, as you put it."

Logan grinned and shook his head with a chuckle. The

easiest way to get Faith to do something was to tell her she couldn't. She was so stubborn and strong-willed, she'd go to the ends of the earth to prove you wrong. It was one of the things he found so incredibly sexy about her.

"Okay then," he said after a moment. "I'll play along, too. The only one who knows the truth is my mom. And your sister and Levi. But something tells me that they're going to have a little too much fun playing along."

She groaned on the other end of the line because she knew he was right. "Okay. I just wanted to make sure we were on the same page."

"Absolutely." Out of the corner of his eye, Logan saw Damon, Nick, and Jeremy coming up the sidewalk. Nice to see that Damon and Jeremy were playing nice after both having a *thing* for Logan's sister. It was all too weird to think about it, but…at least they were past that now.

He waited until they were close enough to overhear before he added, "Go have fun with the girls, Faith. I'll see you at home later. I'll be sure to wake you up when I come in."

He was positive he heard her groan again before he disconnected the call and greeted his new brother-in-law, his new friend, and his old buddy, Jeremy.

"Was that Faith?" Jeremy asked.

He nodded.

"Did you just say what I think you said?"

Logan grinned. "I sure did. She finally came to her senses and saw what a catch I was."

Damon let out a low whistle and shook his head. "I'm impressed," he said. "I wasn't sure I'd ever see the day."

Logan made sure to look directly at Nick, who was new to town and had shown a little more interest in Faith when he'd first arrived in town than Logan would have liked. "I always had faith," he said, fully aware of the play on words.

"Nice." Damon slapped him on the back. "Well, I guess

congratulations are in order," he said as they walked inside to rejoin Brody, who was currently drinking alone.

"Congratulations for what?" he asked as soon as they all sat down.

"For Logan and Faith." Nick raised an eyebrow. "Apparently that article that was going around wasn't fake news after all."

Brody laughed. "I could have told you that. You can't fake chemistry like that."

If they only knew, was his first response. But then again, Brody did have a point. You *couldn't* fake chemistry like that. At least *he* couldn't. And he was pretty sure Faith couldn't either, despite what she was trying to convince herself of.

Chapter Four

FOR STEPHANIE, being in Glacier Falls felt a little like being back in her hometown. Only the town she was raised in was even smaller, and definitely not as friendly. Or maybe that was just the way she was remembering it. Not that it mattered. She hadn't been back home in years, and since her parents had largely distanced themselves from her, there was even less reason to go back. Especially because everyone she'd once considered a friend growing up now only cared about her fame and what she could do for them.

She pulled the curtains back from her hotel room window and looked down at Main Street below. All the people laughing and having fun together. A familiar sense of longing washed over her.

What would it be like to be normal? To have what they had?

As soon as the thoughts filled her head, she pushed them out again. The very idea that she might be ungrateful for what she *did* have was unthinkable. She *was* grateful for her career. She loved acting. She loved traveling the world for her job, for seeing new things, for finally having enough money that she and her parents never had to worry about a thing.

If they'd just let her help them.

Yes. She had so much to be thankful for. And now, she had Dax. And a wedding to look forward to.

According to the media, it would be the wedding of the century.

That seemed a little extreme. And it gave everything a whole new level of pressure, which was exactly what a high-profile celebrity marriage did *not* need. It was hard enough living in the spotlight and having every little move you made examined and publicized for the whole world to see. Thankfully, Dax wasn't like most of the men in Hollywood. He was down-to-earth and real and so completely in love with her. He made her feel safe, and despite their crazy schedules and the ridiculous amount of time they spent away from each other, Stephanie had never once worried that he'd been unfaithful. Maybe she was being naive. Lots of people said so. But…she trusted him. She had to.

Coming from the world of celebrity couples who were constantly cheating and falling in love with their latest costars, there wasn't a lot of choice in the matter. You trusted or you went crazy.

She dropped the curtain and left the window. It was way too nice of a day to spend it inside watching the world go by. Besides, she had told Faith Turner the day before that she'd like to come back to the ranch for more of a visit. She'd really liked her first impressions of the tall blonde woman who seemed so sure of herself and her equally charming boyfriend, who clearly adored Faith. Their banter back and forth was super cute and they'd made her feel at ease right away.

There was almost something familiar about Faith. It was strange, but she'd felt as if she'd met her before, and that almost never happened to Stephanie. As a general rule, she kept people at arm's length for a while before she let them in.

Not that she'd let Faith in, but she would. She could tell. Faith felt like the kind of woman who could actually be a friend. Of course, she was also the wedding planner, and Stephanie had been burned by that type of relationship before.

"No bad energy," she said to herself in the mirror by the door as she jammed a ball cap down on her red hair. "I attract what I put out. Only positive things flow to me."

She still felt a little bit ridiculous every time she said her self-affirmations, but her coach was right; they worked.

Stephanie slipped her sunglasses on, and with her makeshift disguise in place, she set out into town. Before she went out to Ever After Ranch, she wanted to try the bakery that the girl at the front desk had recommended. She'd said the honey buns were to die for, and if the mouthwatering smell coming from the tiny shopfront was any indication, she hadn't been lying.

To hell with her trainer and her nutritionist. One bun couldn't hurt.

And it didn't. Stephanie ate every single crumb of the bun and licked her fingers afterward as she sat in the little park next to the waterfall.

"They're pretty good buns, aren't they?"

Startled, she spun around to see Logan Langdon behind her.

"Sorry," he said. "I didn't mean to scare you. But I saw you sitting over here and thought I'd come say hi. I was just across the street at my sister's shop."

Stephanie's hands immediately went to her hat to be sure it was in place, covering her distinctive red hair.

"Don't worry," Logan said before she could ask anything. "I never would have recognized you if I hadn't met you yesterday."

"Oh, good." Her body instantly relaxed and she smiled.

She knew it was inevitable that she'd be recognized at some point, but until then, it would be nice just to enjoy her time without having a crowd wherever she went. "It's not that I'm… I'm just…"

"I get it." He laughed. "Well, I don't get it because despite my best efforts, I was never able to really convince everyone in Glacier Falls that I was a pretty big deal."

"A legend in your own mind, then?" She laughed, instantly at ease.

He grinned broadly. "You know it."

"Did you say your sister had a shop?" Stephanie changed the subject. She leaned around him, trying to see which one it might be.

"Sure does." Logan pointed. "The Hub. It's brand new, but it's really cool. She rents and sells outdoor equipment so all the visitors we get can go explore the mountains."

"Explore?" Stephanie's eyes opened wide. "Like hike?"

Logan nodded. "And mountain bike and kayak and—"

"Kayak? Like on the river?"

Logan laughed, and even though she was certain he was laughing at her, she didn't care. It had been years since she'd done anything like kayak on a river.

"That's exactly what I mean. There's all kinds of routes, from super chill river floats, to more challenging rapids. But I don't recommend those without a professional guide. Why? You interested?"

He smirked because clearly she was; still, she nodded.

"Absolutely. Do you think I could hire someone to take me?"

Logan's face turned serious and he shook his head. "No."

Her heart sank. Of course. As soon as she found something she was excited about, it wasn't available. She knew she could simply throw money at it and she was absolutely certain she would be able to find someone more than willing to take her out, but before she could offer that as a suggestion, Logan was once again laughing.

"We're not going to charge you to go out alone," he said. "Floating down the river is way more fun in a group. That is, if you're okay with letting one or two people know you're here?"

Chapter Five

"OBVIOUSLY I THINK it's a great idea," Faith said for the third time since Logan had told her his idea of taking Stephanie Starz on a float down the river. "It's been years since I've done a float and it's a super fun time."

"Then what's the issue?"

What was the issue? She tried not to sigh as she looked around the barn at the reception site that had only been half set up for the wedding they were hosting in two days. There was still so much to do, never mind the fact that Hope and Levi were set to arrive on Saturday as well. It was bad enough she wouldn't be there to pick them up from the airport and bring them home. Thankfully, Logan's mom, Debbie, was more than happy to do it. But still, she wanted to—

"Everything will be fine here." Logan interrupted her thoughts. "We can get most of this set up tonight and then after the float, we'll get the last-minute touches ready and it will all be fine."

"It'll be a long night."

"We've had them before." He winked at her and she had to look away.

Mostly because of the annoying flutter his knowing look set off in her tummy. Which was ridiculous, because they'd never had *that* kind of late night together.

Instantly, an image of Logan's naked body hovering over hers flashed through her mind. She flushed and her panties grew damp at the thought of having any kind of late night with Logan that involved him naked in her bed. *After all, it had been awhile since she'd*—no. She shut down her own thought. Maybe she had a little itch to scratch, but even so, Logan was the wrong man for the job. *It would just*—

"Wow. There's a lot going on in your head right now, isn't there?"

Faith blinked hard and cleared her throat in an effort to get back into the moment. "I'm just wondering how we'd…" She let the protest trail away. The truth was, a float down the river *did* sound good, and if it was going to make Stephanie Starz happy, even better. Despite the fact that she was their biggest potential client ever, Faith found herself drawn to the fiery redhead in a way she'd never expected to be. Not that she'd had any expectations about her at all really, except for the fact that her fame was massive and usually with that type of fame came a whole lot of entitlement and snobbery. But not with Stephanie. At least not from what Faith could tell so far.

"Okay," she found herself saying. "Let's do it. But just know we're going to be absolutely exhausted."

Logan grinned and gave her that look that made something deep inside her melt a little. "I'm totally good with it."

The next morning, Logan launched kayaks for both Faith and Stephanie and helped them both get settled in the river. The moment he let go of their boats, he'd regretted it. He should have taken the old canoe out of the shed at his ranch for him and Faith to use. He couldn't think of anything a whole lot better than some forced alone time with her. Unless that alone time was in a bed. But that would come later; he was sure of it.

He watched the two women for a minute, making sure that their celebrity guest was comfortable with her paddle before turning his attention to everyone else. Only a few of their friends had been able to join them on such short notice. Sarah had her daughter, Rory, and the two of them were handling a small canoe together. Damon, of course, had what looked to be like the most expensive, top-of-the-line kayak he'd ever actually seen. Logan tried not to roll his eyes at his new brother-in-law, who had more money than he knew what to do with sometimes, and went to grab his own old, beat-up kayak down from his truck.

"It's too bad Katie couldn't join us," Logan said once he was in the water and paddling next to Damon. "She loves this stuff. "

"She does." Damon dipped his fancy paddle in the water. "But it's pretty busy in the shop and she's still not quite ready to leave things to her new employees. Not entirely. She insisted I come, though, and I'm glad I did. It's a beautiful day for a float. I don't think I've done this since we were kids."

It had been a long time for Logan, too. Despite living right next to the river, it wasn't often that he found the opportunity to actually enjoy it. It was a detail that needed to change. Life was too short to miss out on all the fun. His gaze landed on Faith, who was paddling gently next to Stephanie, engaged in a deep conversation.

Life was definitely too short to miss out on that kind of fun.

"So." Damon's voice interrupted his train of thought before it could really take hold. "I was talking to your mom last night."

Something in the way his brother-in-law spoke made him take note. "You were?"

Damon nodded, a small grin on his face. "We went over for dinner and of course you and Faith came up as a topic of conversation."

"It did, did it?" Logan did not like where this was going. He knew Damon meant well, but despite the fact that he was married to Logan's little sister, and the two of them had been friends since they were young, there was still tension between them at times. Most of it had been resolved when the truth about Katie and Damon's relationship had been revealed, but that was only after they'd had a big fight that had left Katie in tears and one thing Logan couldn't stand was watching his little sister in pain. The two of them seemed to be madly in love and Logan was pretty sure he wouldn't have to worry about that again, but still, his big brother senses were always on high alert. "And what were you saying?" he asked after a moment.

Damon shrugged. "Katie was gushing about how great it was that the two of you had finally come to your senses and realized you were perfect for each other." He looked over at Logan. "You know how she is."

"I do."

"And your mom was actually mostly quiet."

Of course. She knew the truth.

The men had caught a current and the river was rapidly catching them up to where the women were paddling.

"Well, I don't know what to say about that," Logan said as casually as he could. "Mom isn't one to be quiet about much, but maybe—"

"She kind of gave me the impression that she knew something."

Logan's head spun to stare at Damon, who grinned at him. His brother-in-law was starting to get on his nerves. Ahead of them, Stephanie had drifted back a little, and Faith and Sarah were leading the group.

"What would she know?"

Damon took his time answering. "I'm not sure," he finally said as their kayaks caught up with Stephanie's. "Just maybe that you and Faith were—"

"Aren't they the cutest couple?" Stephanie gushed. "Sorry to interrupt," she added quickly. "I wasn't trying to eavesdrop or anything."

"No, it's fine." Logan offered her a charming smile. He wasn't going to let Damon and whatever thoughts he was having ruin what they were trying to do when it came to Stephanie Starz's wedding. Never mind what he was trying to accomplish with Faith. "And you're right," he added. "We are the cutest couple."

Damon groaned.

"It may have taken us a little bit to realize how perfect we are together," Logan continued. He was fully aware that he might be laying it on a little thick, but Stephanie was eating it up and Logan ignored Damon, who was no doubt rolling his eyes. "But now that we've finally come to our senses, I'm never going to let her go. She is the other part of me that I was always missing. You know what I mean?"

"I do! Dax is like that for me," Stephanie said. "I always felt like I was missing something in my life, you know?" She didn't wait for an answer. "I mean, my parents were amazing growing up and while we haven't been close lately, they're good people. I have a career most people would die for. But...I don't know...maybe it was because I was adopted and I never knew who my birth parents were."

"You were adopted?" Damon had maneuvered his kayak so that Stephanie was between them now and, as they let the current carry them gently down the river, only needed to paddle once in a while. "I had no idea. I mean, not that I should know. It just wasn't—"

"It's okay." She saved him. "It's not really well known in the media, small wonder, and it's not something I've ever really thought too much about. I mean, my parents were great growing up, and I don't think I missed out on anything. Not really." She shrugged and once again, her bright smile lit up her face. "But I do think that's why Dax and I are so perfect together. He just makes me feel so…special."

"That's really great," Logan said sincerely. "When is he going to join you? Will we get to meet him before the wedding?" He knew he was pushing it because they didn't officially have her wedding business yet, but he didn't care.

"He's filming in New Zealand right now." Her face once again shadowed, her smile dipping a little. "It's the hardest part about what we do. Being apart. But we're going to make it work." She sounded almost as if she were trying to convince herself and not them, but still, both men nodded and agreed with her. "And that's even more reason why I need a lucky in love wedding venue like Ever After," she continued. "Identical twins both falling madly in love and planning weddings for other brides *with* their partners? It just feels so perfect, you know?"

Logan did.

"I'm so glad I saw that article," she continued. "You and Faith are just…well…it's perfect."

It was perfect. For so many reasons, none of which Logan was going to say. His eyes caught Damon staring at him from across the water, a knowing smirk on his face.

"It is pretty perfect." Damon winked. "Almost like you couldn't have planned for anything more perfect if you'd made it up."

If there hadn't been a person between them, Logan was sure he would have reached over and capsized his brother-in-law for his smug remarks. After all, it wasn't so very long ago he'd faked his own relationship. But Stephanie hadn't seemed to notice anything amiss, and no matter how hard Damon pushed and prodded, Logan wasn't going to admit the truth. If anything, he was going to work that much harder to make it clear that he was madly in love with Faith.

After all, it was pretty damn close to the truth.

Faith hated to admit it, considering it was Logan's idea, but a float down the river was exactly the right thing. It was a gorgeous day. The sun was shining, but with just enough cloud cover to keep them from getting too sunburnt. The water level had come down and the river was moving at a leisurely pace. Just slow enough to look around and enjoy their beautiful surroundings, but fast enough to keep them moving.

It really was a peaceful way to spend the day.

And Stephanie was enjoying it. Which had been the whole point. She'd hardly stopped gushing about how much fun it was to get out and do things in nature and how much she'd missed the Canadian forests and mountains by living down in Los Angeles. There was something about the woman that Faith couldn't help but like. It had started out as a business opportunity, obviously. But it was quickly turning into more of a friendship.

Faith turned as Sarah and her young daughter, Rory, paddled up alongside of her.

"This is so great," Sarah said.

"So fun!" Rory lifted her paddle in the air, sending water raining down on her mother. "I've seen like two deer and three of those big birds with the white heads."

"Bald eagle," her mother supplied.

"Yeah, those."

Faith laughed. "I'm glad you're having fun."

"Can we do this again, Mom? Brody would love it."

"He would," Sarah agreed. "And yes, of course we can do it again."

Faith smiled at them. She'd known Sarah a long time, since they were kids. And she'd known Sarah's first husband—Rory's dad—Josh, too. After Josh died when Rory was only a baby, Sarah had shut down for a long time. It was nice to see that she'd found love again in Brody, who'd proved to be an excellent father figure to Rory, too. Sarah excited about things again, and showing her daughter all of the amazing things their small town had to offer as well instead of hiding.

"It's too bad Brody couldn't join us today," Faith said. "I don't suppose he's paddled a lot of rivers before."

Sarah laughed. "It wouldn't surprise me if he had. But yes, it is too bad. He said there was just too much to do with the wedding tomorrow. Now that he has all the catering for Ever After, he's super busy, especially now that business at Birchwood has picked up, too. He was talking again about hiring some more staff, and that's definitely a good problem to have considering it was only last month that he wasn't sure how he was going to pay all the bills. So as much as I know he'd love to be here today, he's super happy to be busy."

"I can appreciate that."

"In fact," Sarah continued, "I'm surprised that you guys suggested this today. Don't you have a ton of work to do tonight, too? And with Hope and Levi coming home—"

"Don't even get me started." Faith groaned, thinking about all the work they had to do still. It was going to be a very long night getting ready for the wedding the next day. "But having Stephanie Starz in town is kind of a huge opportunity, and when Logan suggested showing her some of what Glacier Falls really had to offer, well…"

"Hey," Sarah said. "I get it. I do. If you guys host this wedding, it will be massive. For everyone. I have to say, you and Logan…you two really are good together."

Faith stiffened. "What do you mean?"

Her friend laughed and shook her head. "It's a compliment, Faith. You two are really good together. You always have been, but now...it's different. You work so well together and you both complement the other one...I don't know how to explain it, but it's like...just perfect. I'm really happy the two of you could finally see it, too. It's nice."

Nice.

Before Faith could think of how to respond, the subject of their discussion called out from somewhere behind them. "Let's stop for lunch soon."

Faith waved in response and navigated her kayak toward the riverbank, and a spit of land that would be perfect to stop and have a picnic on.

She was still mulling over her friend's words as they all hauled their boats up on the shore and Sarah pulled out a cooler full of a delicious lunch Brody had packed for them. *Nice.* It was nice to be with Logan. Annoying and kind of a pain in the ass, but even she had to admit, as the summer wore on and they spent more and more of their time together, it was kind of nice to see him every day and know that when she got out there, he'd already be working on something in the barn. There was always another set of hands to help out, and his cocky smile was ever present. Never mind the way his presence made her stomach flip whenever he was near. Was that *nice?* It was something.

"Hey, babe." Logan sat on the rock next to her and wrapped his arm around her. Before she knew what was happening, he cupped her chin and pulled her in for a long, slow kiss. "I missed you." He grinned. "Have you been avoiding me today?"

Faith shook her head, a little stunned by the impromptu kiss, but then again, Logan was better at this pretending than she was. She shouldn't be surprised. Still, nothing about that kiss felt pretend. "I've been leading the float," she said in response. "How are things at the back of the pack?"

Logan leaned in again and kissed her cheek, using the opportunity to whisper in her ear. "Damon's been asking questions, so I wanted to make sure he knew exactly how serious the two of us are."

Ah. Right. She could play at that game, too.

She lowered her eyelids and turned to him so his lips were only inches from hers. "Oh, we're serious, all right." It was her turn to kiss him, and she didn't waste the opportunity. Aware now that they no doubt had an audience, Faith kissed him with as much passion as was appropriate considering there was a child nearby. Logan moaned against her lips and pulled her closer, so she was pressed up against his chest as much as possible considering the rocks they used as seats. She could feel the heat of him through her T-shirt, and she was thankful for even the thin cloth between them; her kiss had definitely unintended consequences, mostly that she was glad they did in fact have an audience, because the way Logan kissed her back was leaving her breathless and wanting more.

"Enough already!" Damon yelled. "There are children present."

Faith heard Stephanie giggle and then once again gush about how perfect they were as a couple. She didn't know about that, but more and more Faith was starting to think that pretend or not, there was absolutely a heat between them that couldn't be ignored. At least, it couldn't be ignored forever. And more to the point, she wasn't sure she wanted to keep ignoring it.

Chapter Six

IT WAS A FUN DAY, but a long one, and by the time Logan had put the kayaks away, showered, and returned to the barn to finish setting up for the wedding the next day, even he was starting to regret his idea of taking the day off. There really was a lot of work to do. So much, in fact, that Faith had opted to skip her shower altogether and head straight to the barn.

Logan didn't fool himself into thinking that his presence had something to do with her decision. She'd been a little on edge since they'd stopped for lunch on the river and she'd kissed him. And holy shit, had that ever been a kiss. If they'd been alone, he was pretty sure he wouldn't have been able to be held responsible for his actions that without a doubt would have included throwing her over his shoulder and finding the nearest bed, or bed-like surface, so he could show her exactly what the taste of her on his lips did to him.

And he knew she'd felt the same. How could she not? Logan wasn't an inexperienced newbie. He knew when a woman was into him. He could feel it, and every single thing about the way Faith felt, screamed at him that she was just as into him as he was into her.

Fuck.

He was quickly becoming bored of the whole idea of a bet. Win or lose, the only thing he wanted out of the next few weeks was Faith. Of that much he was certain.

Before he'd left the house to return to the barn, he'd pulled together a few quick sandwiches and brewed a fresh pot of coffee. After working with her for the summer, he'd noticed that Faith had a bad habit of not eating. It was probably because she was such a terrible cook, but still, the woman worked her ass off and it was going to be a long night. If she didn't fuel herself properly, it could end badly.

She was ironing tablecloths when Logan found her. They'd planned to get the tables set before they took the day off, but a last-minute change by the bride meant they needed to wash and press all of the pink-peony tablecloths instead of the white that they'd planned to use.

"Only fifteen left to go," Faith said with a groan when she saw him. "I knew we shouldn't have gone today. We have so much to—"

"Hey." Logan put his makeshift picnic on a nearby table that was still empty. "It was worth it. And sometimes we need to remember to have a little fun, right?"

To his surprise, she smiled a little in agreement. "It was fun," she admitted. "It's been way too long since I've done that."

"We should do it more."

We.

He caught himself a moment too late, but she'd noticed his slip. *We.*

Thankfully, she didn't say anything, but only smiled and shrugged, turning back to the tablecloth she was working on. "If you'd asked me four months ago if I'd ever be ironing dozens of tablecloths on a Friday night, I would have laughed in your face." She chuckled and shook her head. "It's crazy how things work out sometimes."

He watched her out of the side of his eye while he poured her a cup of coffee. "For the best?"

She shrugged. "It's definitely different than what I thought," she admitted. "But to be honest, I didn't really have a whole lot going on in the city either, so…this is pretty good." She smiled at him, and it was one of those smiles that was without sass, or judgment, or any of the other things they usually threw at each other. It was fully genuine. And gorgeous.

"Well, I'm glad you're here," he said. And before she could get her back up because he was being too mushy or whatever else she'd call him out for, he added, "Come eat. I made you a sandwich, and if you don't eat it I'll take it as a personal offense."

"You'll take it that way anyway," she fired back. But despite the fire, she actually put the iron down, folded the tablecloth and joined him at the table. She smiled in what he took as an appreciative gesture and took a big bite of her sandwich.

Logan held his and watched her while she ate. Her eyes closed, enjoying every single bite of what was just a basic ham and cheese sandwich. Had it really been so long since someone had made her a sandwich? Had *anyone* ever made her a sandwich? Faith was a fierce, strong, and independent woman, but that didn't mean she couldn't use a little someone taking care of her once in a while. And dammed if Logan didn't find himself wanting to be that man.

The feelings were all completely new to him.

Mostly.

Never in his life had Logan cared more about a woman than simply taking her out to impress her with a nice dinner or maybe a movie if they were in the city, just so he could get her into bed. There had only ever been one woman who'd made him want more. But she'd never reciprocated the feelings.

Ever.

Except... Maybe...just maybe...that was starting to change.

Faith opened her eyes and saw him staring at her. "What?" She self-consciously wiped at her chin. "Do I have mustard on my face?" She swiped again.

"No." He shook his head and smiled. "I was just watching you."

"Why?" She instantly looked suspicious.

What was it about this woman that she always had her guard up? If she hadn't been so on edge when they were younger, he might have been able to make her see back then what he thought about her.

He kept his eyes soft and shook his head slightly. "Because you're gorgeous."

"Stop it." She wiped her face again and took a swallow of her coffee before getting up from the table. "There's no one here, Logan. You don't have to—"

He stopped her with a kiss. He wasn't going to let her walk away from him. Not again. She was tense in his arms, but it only took a moment for her whole body to melt into his touch. When he pulled away, her eyes were heavy with desire, her breath coming in short pants. Slowly, she looked up at him, blinking hard.

"Faith, you should know by now, I only do things because I want to."

It was a bad idea. It was all a bad idea.

Logan's kisses made her feel things. And getting involved with Logan—at least more than they already were—was a bad idea. No. It was a friggin' terrible idea. It was literally the one thing she'd spent her entire adult life avoiding. Logan made her want things she shouldn't want. Things that weren't realistic.

Things that couldn't be real. At least not for any length of time. The only thing that would come from letting Logan make her feel something was heartache.

Or…

Maybe there was something else? Maybe Logan could give her the release she was so desperately looking for? After all, she was a grown-ass woman. She could keep things casual. Just sex. Why not? Besides, it would help with the whole optics of the situation.

"It wouldn't kill you to relax a little, Faith."

And just like that, Faith remembered why Logan would *never* be a good idea.

She blinked hard, and shook her head. "Fuck you, Logan." She pulled away and grabbed another tablecloth off the pile.

"Faith, that's not what I—"

"We have work to do, Logan, and I don't want to be here all night because you thought that taking the day off was a good idea."

"Faith, don't do—"

"Do what, Logan?" She put the iron down, turned and glared at him. "Don't do my job? Don't try my best to pull off this gorgeous wedding when I'm already exhausted? Or maybe you mean, don't try to win this stupid bet that you forced me into so I can get rid of you once and for all."

She could see that her words hit him. He physically took a step back and for an instant, pain flashed on his face. She thought he might argue with her, challenge her even more than he already had. She was ready for it. Hell, she *wanted* him to. Faith braced herself when Logan took a breath and opened his mouth.

But then he closed it again without saying a word. He turned, grabbed the stack of freshly ironed tablecloths, and started to set up the tables at the opposite end of the barn, leaving Faith wanting and feeling oddly disappointed.

She made him crazy. She made him *fucking* crazy. And she had no idea the power she had over him. He hated it. But at the same time, he craved it. She was the biggest challenge of his life and just when he thought he was getting somewhere with her, getting through to her so she could finally understand that what he wanted with her was so much more than a *bet* or a *screw* or whatever else she thought he wanted from her—just when Logan thought she understood and maybe, just maybe she felt the same way—she pulled away.

No. She *ran* away.

He'd never seen a woman so fucking afraid of letting someone else in. She'd always been that way, too. How was it that she could be so bloody different from her identical twin sister? Hope had always led with love. Her heart was wide open and ever since they were kids, she believed wholeheartedly in the idea of happily ever after. Even when Logan's cousin Levi had broken her heart and left her behind, she never stopped believing.

And then there was Faith. Something had happened to her along the way to make her cynical and hard. But for the life of him, he couldn't figure it out. And he'd spent most of his life trying. When she moved away after high school, he'd thought that once and for all he'd get her out of his system. After all, out of sight, out of mind. Logan had almost thought himself successful, too. But all it had taken was one look at her, one word off her sharp tongue, and he was totally lost again.

They spent the next few hours working in silence, getting the wedding set up. After almost a whole summer of it, they worked pretty well together and it didn't take nearly as long as he'd thought. Still, when the last napkin was folded, they were both exhausted.

Ever since Logan had forcibly moved into her house, he'd

slept on the couch in the living room. Moving in unannounced had been a bold move, even for him, but he was pretty sure he would have been pushing it to try to snuggle up with her right away. Although he would have been more than happy to, and it had always been the goal. Still, he didn't want to push her too hard, too fast.

The silence between them had only grown thicker as Logan followed Faith up to her room so he could brush his teeth. He saw her watching him. Maybe she was waiting for him to speak first. Make the first move after what she'd said to him in the barn.

Trying to win the bet.

He couldn't pretend those words hadn't hurt. Especially because he knew they weren't true. He knew in his heart that this wasn't just about a bet. It couldn't be.

She was waiting outside the bathroom when he came out. She'd changed into the shorts and T-shirt he'd come to know were her pajamas. The shirt was a size too small and hugged her breasts tightly, outlining every single curve. Logan's body reacted to the sight of her, his cock twitching in his pants.

"Okay," she said. "Thanks for all your help tonight. I'll see you in the morning." She moved to walk past him. No doubt she assumed he'd excuse himself to the couch the way he had every other night. But something about her standing there watching him the way she was, and the way she'd spoken to him in the barn earlier, had shifted something.

He moved to block her path into the bathroom and pressed an arm against the wall behind her, framing her in with his body. Her eyes grew wide, and her breath came quick. Logan let his eyes drift down to her breasts straining against the tight shirt. Her hard nipples formed two perfect peaks under the cotton and he yearned to reach out and touch them. Cup her breasts in his hands and roll each nipple in turn between his thumb and finger. Just thinking of it made his cock grow thick between his legs.

His voice was low and gruff as he leaned in so he was only inches from her mouth. "I'm not sleeping on the couch tonight, Faith."

She opened her mouth, no doubt to protest, but he wasn't going to give her the chance. His lips pressed to hers and his free hand slid up her body, just resting under the swell of her breast. He fanned his fingers out, needing to touch as much of her as possible.

A low moan escaped her throat, and he swallowed it down as he kissed her deeper. Enough was enough. Whatever it was that was going on between them, it was more than time for this.

Logan pressed his body against her hips, pinning her to the wall so he could free up both hands to travel the length of her. This time, he slipped his fingers under the cotton of her shirt and pulled it up as he moved. She didn't protest, but only groaned again, deeper, as her knees buckled a little. He lifted the cotton up and over her breasts and, needing to savor the moment, pulled away from her mouth, long enough to take in the sight of what were the most beautiful tits he'd ever seen in his life.

He'd always known she was perfect, but to see her for the first time was something else. It was his turn to groan. His need for her was unmatched. "Fuck, Faith. You're fucking gorgeous."

Again, he didn't wait for her to respond, afraid she'd pull away or run again, not letting herself have this. His mouth crashed to hers once more, in a kiss more intense and demanding than ever before as his hands cupped each of her breasts. Just as he'd imagined, they filled his palms perfectly. She groaned and squirmed beneath him, and when he took

ELENA AITKEN

each nipple between his thumb and fingers and pinched, just a little, her knees buckled.

"Logan...I..."

He pulled away so he could look her in the eyes. Her lids were heavy, her lips parted and slightly swollen from their kisses. Her breath came in short pants, and he'd never seen her looking sexier.

He held his breath, willing her not to push him away, but knowing that if she said the word, he'd walk out of her room and sleep on the couch.

She swallowed hard and looked him in the eye. "This doesn't mean you won."

Logan's stomach flipped and his lips curved up into a grin. "Of course not."

She threw herself forward and kissed him hard. Her hands slid under his shirt and lifted it up. He pulled back long enough to let her yank it up over his head and toss it behind him before her mouth was on his again. It was his turn to groan.

He moved his mouth down her neck, kissing and biting, sure that he was leaving a mark behind, but he didn't care—and judging by the sexy noises she made, she didn't care either.

He needed her shirt gone. He tugged it up and over her head. Her long blonde hair fell in gentle waves, just covering the tips of her breasts. Still up against the wall, he bent and sucked one nipple into his mouth. He bit down gently, but enough to get a reaction out of her. She wiggled beneath him and pressed her hips into him.

"Damn, woman."

Logan took a step back so he could slip a hand between them and into her tiny sleeping shorts. Just as he'd known she would be, she was wet and ready. He would have liked to take his time, but the heat building between them wasn't going to allow for it. He pressed one finger inside her moist heat and she groaned.

"Oh my God, Logan. I—"

He pressed another finger inside her, cutting off the words before they could form. "Were you saying something?"

Her mouth hung open as the pleasure built inside her, and it was the sexiest thing he'd ever seen. He kissed her again, overwhelming her senses as he moved his fingers inside her, gently pulling them out to circle her throbbing clit before pressing them back inside. Her orgasm hit hard as she came undone around his hand, moaning out her release into his kiss.

Fuck. There was no way once was going to be enough with her. Ever.

He waited a few seconds for her to regain her senses. She stood against the wall, panting for breath, her eyes still closed as Logan quickly shed himself of his jeans and shimmied her shorts down and over her hips. Her eyes opened and caught him watching her, nothing but appreciation on his face for what was the most beautiful woman he'd ever laid eyes on. The slight flush of her skin from her orgasm, the way her breasts heaved with every hot breath she took—everything about her was absolutely gorgeous.

He shook his head a little. "Dammit, Faith."

"What? What is it?" Concern crossed her face and she moved to step away from the wall, but Logan put both of his hands on her hips to stop her.

"I need you, Faith. I need you so badly."

Easily, Logan picked her up.

She smiled at his words and licked her bottom lip a little as she wrapped her legs around him in response.

He knew he should walk her a few steps over to the bed, but he was pretty sure he wouldn't be able to make it. He needed her with every fiber of his being.

Logan lifted her hips a little and slid his length into her, taking her hard against the wall. He held himself, his eyes closed, enjoying every sensation that washed over him.

But not for long. Because he hadn't been lying when he said how badly he needed her. She groaned and he moved, pulling back just to enter her again. And again.

Their lovemaking was hot and hard, and when finally, Logan's own climax started to build, he felt her begin to shake with another of her own. They crested together, screaming out their release.

When he finally regained his senses long enough, Logan carried her, still wrapped around him, to the bed, where he pulled her close and wrapped his body around her.

Faith fell into a deep sleep almost at once, her breath coming slow and even, but Logan was no longer tired. He stroked her hair and let his hands slide over her body, memorizing every curve. Being with Faith had been more than he'd ever imagined, and that scared the hell out of him. Because now that he'd had her, he wasn't ever going to want to let her go.

Chapter Seven

STEPHANIE READ the headline on the gossip site again.

"Dax Combs stepping out?"

It didn't matter how many times she read it; the words still blurred in front of her and made her stomach roll.

Stepping out?

Dax wouldn't cheat on her. No way. She had to trust him. Without trust, they had nothing. She knew that. The accompanying picture was one of him and his current costar Natalie Fear. They were simply standing close together, nothing more. There was nothing to indicate that he was cheating on her, or that the photo was anything more than a shot of the two of them on set together.

Still.

It left her unsettled. Particularly because they hadn't been able to connect on the phone much lately. The time difference made it hard, and of course Dax's demanding shooting schedule. They'd mostly stopped trying to get each other on a video call and had instead moved to sending each other lengthy text messages. The last time she'd actually spoken to him on the phone was the day before she'd made the trip to Glacier Falls, when she'd told him where she would be. He was the only one who thought her trip was a good idea. Especially because she was going alone and had turned down offers from her agents, assistant, and various other staff members to accompany her.

Dax had understood her desire to do it on her own. He understood how much she hated the fame at times. That was one of the things that helped them connect. He *got* it. Because he, too, had told her he would have traded in his entire career for a quieter lifestyle. They'd even discussed what that would look like. The two of them, retiring and settling somewhere where no one knew them, to build a life and raise a family.

It could look like living in Glacier Falls.

She'd only been in town a few days, but she was already totally in love. Faith and Logan had welcomed her so completely, and their friends too. No one treated her like she was different. Not one of them had asked anything from her. Except, of course, for the fact that she knew hosting her wedding would be a huge boost to Ever After Ranch. But never once had Stephanie felt as though that were the only reason Faith and Logan had befriended her.

For the first time since she was young, she felt as if she were a part of something.

Which was going to make it even harder to leave.

Reluctantly, she picked up her phone from the desk and saw she had four missed calls. One from her agent and three from her assistant, Terri.

There'd been a time when she'd actually thought of Terri as her closest friend. And although she was a really great assistant, that's all she was. An assistant. Stephanie paid her to be her friend. The thought made her sad. Especially now that she'd spent some time with Faith and Sarah. That was true friendship.

She contemplated returning the calls, but the idea of it exhausted her. Terri would just want to know when she was coming home and no doubt, Brenda, her agent, would want an answer about the latest script she'd sent over. The one that was still in her bag because she hadn't looked at it yet.

Before Stephanie could put her phone down, it rang in her hand. The sound jarred her from the quiet. But her surprise quickly turned to pleasure when she saw Dax's face on the screen.

"Hey," she said as she answered the call. "What time is it? It must be the middle of the night there?"

"It is." His warm voice reached through the line from the other side of the world. "But I missed hearing your voice, so I set an alarm."

He did sound a little groggy, but she loved him all the more for thinking of her and making the sacrifice. "I miss you."

"I miss you too, babe. So much," he said. "I still wish you would have come with me."

There'd been more than one occasion when she'd wished she would have gone with him, too. But she knew from experience that it wasn't a vacation to visit your partner on set. They worked long hours and were often completely consumed by the shoot and had very little time for anything extra. Including spending time with anyone who wasn't involved in the production.

Dax and Stephanie had made a decision early on not to get involved with each other's work. It was a decision they'd both had opportunity to regret, but by and large it had been the right choice.

"You'll be done soon, Dax."

"I will," he said. "You know I love you, babe, right?" There was something in his voice.

"Dax? What's wrong?"

"The article," he said simply. "You know it's bullshit, right?"

They'd been here before. Plenty of times. With fame like

theirs, almost no week went by without some trashy tabloid site publishing some garbage about one or both of them. "I know," she said with as much confidence as she could muster. "But it always stings a little to see it."

"I know, I know." His voice soothed her. "And it makes it even harder to be apart. But you're all I think about, babe. Every day, all day."

She believed him. The same way he believed her every time some garbage was published about her.

"Tell me about this town you've found. Your text messages make it sound like a little bit of paradise. Will I like it?"

"You'll love it. In fact…" The idea came to her while Dax had been speaking, and she probably should have thought about it a bit more, and let it mull over in her brain a bit, but she couldn't help it. She blurted it out. "I think we should get married here."

He laughed. "I thought that was the plan all along?"

"I know, I know. But I mean right away. Like a quickie elopement. You're almost done there, right? You can just come straight here and we can do it, just the two of us before the press finds out."

He was silent for a moment. "An elopement? I thought you wanted the big wedding with the big white dress and—"

"Not anymore." She hadn't even realized it herself, but just by spending time in Glacier Falls and meeting all of Faith and Logan's friends, who had their own amazing wedding stories, none of which were traditional, her opinion had started to change. "I just think there's something so magical about this town, I can't even explain it. And more than that, it's private. No press." Her thoughts went back to the photo of Dax and his costar. The tabloids were going to be the death of her. "I'm treated like a normal person here, Dax. No reporters following me around and questioning my every move. It's nice. And if we could get married without all of that…well, then, I think we should."

"This will make you happy?"

"Very."

"Let's do it then."

She squealed and clapped her hands as Dax laughed on the other end of the line.

"I'll talk to Faith about it and we'll organize all the details, okay? You'll be here next week?"

"I can be there by Wednesday."

"That's in five days!"

"Too soon?"

"No way."

They spent the next fifteen minutes discussing Glacier Falls and the people she'd met. She told him all about Ever After and the weddings Faith and Logan held, throwing in suggestions for their own super private and quiet nuptials. She talked as long as she could, with Dax agreeing it sounded amazing as his voice got more and more distant.

"You're falling asleep," she finally said. "I should let you go. You probably have an early call tomorrow."

"I am and I do. I love you, Steph. I'll see you soon."

She stared at the quiet phone long after they hung up. It had been good to hear his voice, but in some ways it just made the loneliness worse.

Chapter Eight

EVERY SINGLE WEDDING Faith had been in charge of in the last few months had some glitch of some kind: A torn hem on a bridesmaid's dress. An intoxicated groom. A photographer who didn't show up. Or arguing in-laws. She'd seen a lot, but she hadn't yet seen a missing bride. Of course, that particular extra-special problem would present itself the day she was operating on very little sleep with her pregnant and sick sister due home, and the sexual tension between her and Logan so thick that she couldn't even look at him without blushing.

Somehow Faith managed to calm down the bride's parents, keep the groom from knowing his bride was missing, *and* track down the woman who didn't have cold feet at all, but instead a flat tire in her bridesmaid's car on the way from the city. It was a stressful day, to say the least, but at least it kept her busy, which kept her from thinking. Which was a good thing, because when she did have a quiet moment to think, her thoughts went directly to Logan. And the way he'd touched her, kissed her, and made her moan the night before. More than once.

She'd fallen asleep in his arms, completely content and

exhausted from their passionate lovemaking, but she hadn't been asleep very long when his touches had woken her again. He'd made love to her then slowly, from behind, half awake. He'd held her close, his arms keeping her in place as he kissed her neck and made her come again and again.

Just remembering the tender way he'd kissed her made her long for his touch again.

Earlier that morning, as the sun came up, they'd had a quick coupling. Almost frantic, as if once the night was over, so was their time together. And maybe it was.

After all, it wasn't real.

It had been a mistake to let it happen at all. Faith couldn't let it happen again. She couldn't get used to being with him as if it were anything more than a stupid arrangement. A short-lived, stupid arrangement that would not only land her the biggest wedding and *huge* business for Ever After but would also help her win the bet that would get Logan Langdon to finally leave her alone for good.

And that's what she wanted.

Right?

Somehow, it didn't feel like what she wanted anymore.

Not after what they'd shared the night before. That had felt…like trouble, was what it felt like.

Faith stood behind the bar and leaned against the door to the kitchen as she watched the groom toast his new bride. It had been a beautiful wedding. Their vows had been special and personal, and had even brought a tear to Faith's eye. That almost never happened. Although, she couldn't help but notice it was happening a little more often lately.

She felt him before she saw him. It had been such a busy day, they'd only barely crossed paths and hadn't spoken any words to each other that weren't directly related to the event at hand.

He stood close but didn't touch her. "That was a close one today, wasn't it?"

She nodded but didn't turn. "I'm not going to lie, I thought we might have a runaway bride on our hands."

"But you pulled it off, Faith. It was beautiful."

Something about his voice sent a slow shiver through her, almost as if he'd touched her. Her body yearned for him. If she'd thought she'd got enough of him last night, the way her body vibrated just by having him close made it painfully clear that she hadn't.

When he finally, lightly traced his fingers down her back, Faith's instinct was to lean back against him and into his arms. It would be so easy to let Logan wrap his arms around her and pull her tight. But nothing with Logan was easy.

She needed to remember that.

Faith took a step to the side and Logan's arm dropped.

"It's like that, is it?"

It wasn't like that. At least, she didn't want it to be like that. But with Logan, was there any other way?

"Look." She dropped her head. "It's been a long day, and I don't think that this is the time or the place to do this, okay?"

He looked affronted. "*This?* What exactly is *this*, Faith?"

She shook her head, exhausted. "Logan, it's not—"

"Don't do this, Faith. Don't do what you always do."

She spun on him. It took a great effort, but she kept her voice low, aware that they were in the middle of a wedding. "And what is it that I always do?"

"You run, Faith. As soon as something starts to get good, you run."

She bristled.

"You're allowed to feel good," he continued. "You're allowed to feel love, to feel—"

"This isn't love," she hissed.

He recoiled and she instantly regretted her choice of

words. Maybe it wasn't love. Maybe it was just...*fuck*. Either way, she'd hurt him and she could see it.

"I don't know what happened to you," he spat. "I don't know who hurt you or what went down that was so bloody catastrophic that caused you to shut the fucking door on your heart, but it's a goddammed tragedy, Faith. You and I, we could be—"

"Nothing, Logan." She steeled herself and looked past him. "We could be nothing, Logan. We never were, and we never could be."

She felt every word in her gut as she spoke them. Felt every word as they hit him hard. When Logan took a step away from her with a look of bewilderment on his face, she had to force herself not to react. Because she'd meant what she said. They could be nothing. And whether he wanted to admit it or not, Logan knew she was right. They'd only ever been adversaries. Flirts...nothing more. Never a relationship. How could they?

Faith watched as he shook his head, not even bothering to hide the wounded expression on his face. "You don't mean that, Faith."

She swallowed hard. A vision of her parents—who were supposed to be more in love than anyone else—flashed in her memory. They were yelling at each other. Saying terrible, awful things. Was that love? Was that what it was supposed to be?

No thank-you.

She'd sworn right then never to subject herself to that kind of hurt. She'd seen the way her mother had recoiled at her father's words. The pain in her chest. The hurt he'd caused her. All because of words from the man who was supposed to love her more than anyone else in the world.

No.

Faith vowed never to let herself feel that way. Never let herself be that kind of vulnerable.

Never.

She looked at Logan and her heart seized. Things had changed. *She* had changed. And there was more than once that Faith had questioned why she'd be holding on so long to her long-ago beliefs on how terrible it would be to release her heart to someone else. She'd considered more than once that she'd actually been wrong all this time to keep her heart closed off. And for a moment, Faith thought she might give in and tell Logan that she did care about him. That she did…

He waited and watched her, his expression vulnerable and even a little hopeful, but ultimately, she couldn't do it.

Faith shook her head and looked away. "I'm sorry, Logan."

"It's so good to see you, Levi." Logan pulled his cousin in for a hug and slapped his back. It had only been a few months, but it *was* good to see him again. They'd been so close once, and despite years apart when Levi had left home to work on fishing boats on the ocean, the two of them were like brothers. "But I'm so sorry your trip got cancelled early. I know you guys were hoping to see—"

"Doesn't matter, man." Levi waved away his concern. "None of it matters except having Hope healthy and safe with our baby."

"Oh, shit. That's right." Logan smacked his palm to his forehead. "With everything, I completely forgot. Congratulations are definitely in order."

His cousin's face lit up and Logan couldn't help but smile, too. Levi and Hope had taken the long road to get back to each other, but it was great to see them finally together and married the way they always should have been. And now that they were starting a family, everything was that much more perfect.

"Thanks, Logan. And honestly, I know what the doctors said, but I think I'm a whole lot more comfortable being back in town for Hope's pregnancy. There's just too many things that can go wrong. I feel better here."

That's right. Logan had largely forgotten about Hope's cancer diagnosis. It was easy to forget, because just looking at her, it was hard to reconcile the bright, outgoing, full of life woman he knew so well was dealing with a life-altering cancer diagnosis. It was a fight that would resume full force as soon as the baby was born. But Levi was right; it was probably best to have her home and in close reach of the doctors. He knew that's what Faith had always wanted as well.

Faith.

His mood changed in a flash at the thought of the woman. She was infuriating. How one woman could be so goddammed conflicted about what she wanted was beyond him.

"Hey, what's up?" Levi looked at him sideways. "You are happy to have us back, right?"

Logan nodded. "Yes," he said pointedly. "Very happy. But, man, do I have a lot to fill you in on."

Levi laughed. "Is that going to include why exactly you're living here right now? And maybe why Faith looked like she was ready to stab you a minute ago when you both walked in?"

Logan exhaled hard. He was pretty sure he'd never be able to explain *that* to his cousin, but he could certainly let him in on the details of everything else. It didn't matter that it was already way past midnight; it had been way too long since the men had caught up. Over the next hour, and a handful of beers each, Logan told Levi exactly what was going on between him and Faith—at least to the best of his ability to explain it—starting with the news article, which he already knew about, and the bet he'd used to trick Faith into pretending to be his girlfriend and finishing with his concussion over the cold shoulder she'd given him after they'd spent what could only be described as an amazing night together.

"I don't know what to tell you, man." Levi shook his head.

"I love Faith, she's like my sister, but as much as her and Hope share similarities, there are a few things where they are fundamentally different, and I have no idea why that is."

Logan dropped his head into his hands, the exhaustion of the long day, lack of sleep, and the effects of a few beers finally starting to take their toll. "I don't know either, Levi. I really don't. I thought I'd been getting through to her. Finally cracking that tough shell, but…I'm starting to think it can't be done. At least not by me."

Levi got up from the table and smacked him on the shoulder before giving it a squeeze. "Don't give up, Logan. Some of the very best things in life are worth fighting for. I gotta go to bed. Jet lag is going to be a killer. I'll see you in the morning."

Logan lifted his head.

"Don't stay up too late driving yourself crazy, okay?"

Logan nodded, but he couldn't make any promises. It was going to be another long night on the couch, because there was no way he could imagine Faith letting him share her bed again and he wasn't sure he had the energy to push her.

Faith lay awake in bed. Once in a while, Levi and Logan's voices would drift up the stairs to her, but she couldn't make out what they were saying. Not that she needed to. There was no doubt in her mind that Logan was sharing all the gory details of their…whatever it was. She sighed and tried not to let it bother her, especially because she planned to share all of those very same details with her sister the first chance she had.

Before she'd gone to bed, Faith had checked in on Hope, who was already set up in her room, having arrived home from the airport while Faith and Logan were still working the wedding in the barn. Hope's eyes had fluttered open a little and she'd smiled when she'd seen her sister, but she was clearly exhausted, and given the late hour, Faith didn't want her to feel like she had to stay up. So they'd had a quick hug and Faith had left her to sleep. There would be lots of time for talking now that she was home.

She was still lying awake, unable to shut her mind off long enough to sleep, when she heard the bedroom door open. She stiffened, and tried to hold her breath as Logan moved quietly past the bed and into the attached bathroom.

There was no way he was going to try to crawl in next to her. He wouldn't dare. Not after their argument in the barn. During *the event.* She shook her head. That had been so ridiculously unprofessional. She had to try harder to keep their personal life outside of that barn. Especially during events, or it wouldn't matter whether they hosted Stephanie Starz's wedding or not—their reputation would be shot. No bride wanted another couple causing drama in the middle of her wedding. Especially the wedding planners.

A few minutes later, Faith heard the toilet flush, and the bathroom door opened. She lay on her side in the dark. Her eyes were open a crack, but she was sure that Logan couldn't see her. He paused at the foot of the bed and for a moment, she was sure he was going to pull the covers back and get in. She could say something. Let him know she wasn't asleep and he wasn't welcome in her bed.

But at the same time…wasn't he?

Conflicted feelings raced through her. It was so easy to be angry and keep him at arm's length. It was like a reflex. But letting him in, that had been nice too. *More* than nice. Making love with Logan had been unlike anything else she'd ever experienced. It had been every single cliché she'd ever heard. She'd heard it before, but never believed it. Maybe sex really was even better with someone you cared about? Maybe she *did* care about Logan. Maybe she—

Logan sighed loudly, turned, and walked away.

As the door clicked shut softly behind him, Faith let out the breath she'd been holding and an overwhelming sense of loss filled her. Her bed seemed a little bit bigger all of a sudden. And colder. And as she wrapped her arms around herself, she felt a little bit lonelier, too.

Chapter Nine

SOMEWHERE BEYOND HIS DREAM, Logan heard the knock on the door, followed by voices. Vaguely, he recognized that he should probably get up, but after tossing and turning most of the night, he'd finally fallen into a deep sleep and the last thing he wanted to do was—

"Logan? Oh, I'm sorry. I—"

He jumped to his feet. The blanket fell down onto the couch, leaving him standing in only his boxer briefs as he turned to see Stephanie Starz in the living room.

Shit.

"Hey." He rubbed his hand over his face and searched his brain for words that would make sense in the situation, but nothing came to him. "I was just—"

"I'm so sorry to...well...I didn't mean to wake you...I just..."

"No," he said quickly as he reached for his T-shirt and jeans, tugging both pieces of clothing on. "You're fine. I was just—"

"Oh, there you are." Levi appeared behind her in the hall. His eyes were wide and behind her, he shook his head in a sort of apology to Logan, although it was clear he had no idea what he was apologizing for. "I just ran up to see if Hope was awake yet," he said in explanation. "I didn't realize that Logan was…well, why don't we sit down in the kitchen and visit instead."

Fuck. Fuck. Fuck.

Faith had said something to him about how she'd told Stephanie that Levi and Hope were coming home and because the star was so excited to meet them both, she'd told Stephanie to come over for a coffee in the morning and…*fuck.* He'd completely forgotten and now…

"That sounds great," Logan said as smoothly as he could. "I'll go see if my love is awake yet." He knew he was laying it on thick, and judging by the way Levi rolled his eyes, his cousin also had an opinion. "It was so late last night when we were done catching up that I hadn't wanted to wake her up, so I just slept down here." It was a lame excuse, but it would have to do.

Stephanie's face still read a mixture of horror at waking him up and confusion, because why would a couple who was supposed to be madly in love be sleeping separately? Logan knew exactly how it looked. *Shit.*

Before she could say anything more, Logan grabbed up the blanket, pasted a grin on his face, and quickly excused himself. He took the stairs two at a time.

Faith was already up, and dressed. Her hair was wrapped up in a towel, and fresh from the shower, she was gorgeous. For a minute, he forgot why he'd barged in so frantically. Faith turned and stared at him. For a minute, her face screwed up into a frown, and he was sure she was going to yell at him.

Logan held his hands up and before she had a chance to say anything, he said, "Stephanie's here."

Her face registered the problem quickly as she took in the blanket in his hand, and his rumpled appearance.

"You slept on the couch."

It wasn't a question. But still, he answered it, his voice low.

"I didn't think you would want me to…"

She looked away but didn't say a word.

"It doesn't matter." He moved across the room to her, and tossed the blanket on the bed. "She walked in on me sleeping. I told her I didn't want to disturb you by coming to bed so late, but I don't know if—"

"Shit."

He couldn't help but chuckle. "That's what I said."

"I forgot that I invited her over this morning." Faith pulled the towel from her hair and combed her fingers through the wet locks. "I just didn't think you were going to…it doesn't matter."

It did.

"You didn't think I'd what?"

"I told you," she said. "It doesn't matter. I need to get down there. I did invite her over, after all, and Hope will be…" Her face shifted into a brilliant smile. "I didn't even get a chance to talk to her last night, she was so tired."

Logan couldn't help but be touched by their closeness. As happy as he was to see Levi, he knew it was nothing compared to the bond between the twins. "Well, now she's here again and the good news about that is that you have plenty of time together."

Faith stopped what she was doing and looked at him with a soft smile. "That's exactly it." But then the smile was gone, replaced again by the frantic look in her eyes. "I can't believe she saw you on the couch. Do you think she believed it? Do you think she knows?" Faith shook her head without waiting for an answer. "We never should have tried to—"

He cut her off with a kiss. Logan had to work hard to keep the kiss chaste enough that he didn't want to throw her back on the bed and show her exactly what she'd been missing, sleeping alone.

When he pulled away. Faith was breathless, but only for a minute.

Then she looked as if she might straight up punch him. "What the hell, Logan?"

He smiled as innocently as he could. "I thought maybe when you go downstairs it would help if you were a little flushed with that *just thoroughly kissed* look, that's all." He stepped back and looked her up and down, which he knew would make her crazy annoyed. "Mission accomplished."

Before she could respond, or more likely, hit him, he squeezed past her and into the bathroom. Faith was right; she needed to get downstairs. And he needed to shower up and join them.

But first he needed to slow his pulse and cool his blood, because *damn* that woman. Even when she was mad enough to hit him, she turned him completely inside out.

"Stephanie!" Faith ran into the kitchen. There'd been no time to brush her hair out properly, let alone put any makeup on. It was bad enough she'd slept in, and with Logan on the couch… she didn't even want to think about it. The lie they'd told was bad, definitely, but now that they were in it, it would be even worse if they got discovered in such a terrible way. Stephanie did seem to be an understanding person, but no one liked to be lied to and the publicity from that…no way. She wasn't going to risk it. "I'm so sorry I wasn't down here to greet you." Faith gave Stephanie a quick hug.

"Not to worry." Her smile was sweet and she genuinely didn't seem to be upset by the delay. "Besides, it gave me a chance to get to know Levi, who makes a delicious cup of coffee."

"It's not me." Levi grinned. "It's all in the beans. I can't take any actual credit."

"I don't know." Faith laughed as she poured herself a cup. "I think it must be genetic because Logan has mad coffee skills, too."

At the mention of Logan, Stephanie's smile dipped and there was a question in her eyes. "I didn't mean to wake him up this morning," she said. "I didn't know he was—"

"It's totally fine." Faith waved away her apology. "He should have just come up to bed last night. Sometimes I think he's a little too thoughtful. He's more embarrassed than anything else."

From behind her, she heard Levi choke on a laugh, but she ignored him and looked to Stephanie instead. "Has Levi been filling you in on all the romantic details of his own love story with my sister?"

Levi laughed. "I'll leave all the gory details up to you women," he said. "In fact, I was just going to go get Hope and set her up in the living room, if you're ready for a visit."

Faith spun around. "I thought she needed to stay on bed rest?"

"It's not strict." Levi nodded seriously. "At least not yet. She's supposed to spend as much time resting as possible to keep her blood pressure down, but if we make sure she has comfortable places to rest down here, I think that will probably help with morale so she doesn't go too stir-crazy upstairs alone."

"Makes sense." Stephanie nodded. "A friend of mine... well, she was more of a costar, I guess...was on bed rest with her last pregnancy, and she had a receiving room set up in her house so guests could come and..." She drifted away, not finishing the thought. "I realize how pretentious that sounds. I mean, her house in Hollywood was...never mind."

Faith offered her new friend the kindest smile she could. "It's okay," she said. "That's your life. Don't feel bad for it."

"The thing is, it's not my life." The ever-present smile on the other woman's face was gone, replaced by a sad frown. "It kind of became my life," she continued. "But it still doesn't feel right."

Faith noticed Levi slip from the room. No doubt he recognized a deep female conversation in the works and took the moment to make his escape. His instincts were right, because only seconds after he'd left, Stephanie dropped her head to the table and started to cry. Faith sat frozen, unsure of what to do, but only for a second before jumping up and fetching the box of tissues. She slid it in front of the other woman and pulled up a chair so she was sitting closer.

"I'm sorry." Stephanie lifted her head and grabbed at the tissues, wiping her face and blowing her nose loudly. "I'm not sure what just came over me. I barely even know you and it's not fair to dump my drama on you. I'm just..." She dissolved into tears again.

Faith sat quietly, waiting her out. She'd never been much of a crier, but Hope had been, especially when they were younger, and the best thing she could do was sit with her and let her cry out her feelings.

It took a little longer than she thought, but soon enough, Stephanie sat up and wiped her eyes again. She shook her head and apologized again and again, but there was no need.

"Honestly," Faith said gently. "It's okay. You don't need to apologize. Sometimes we get emotional. It's totally normal." Stephanie gave her a look and Faith smiled. "Really. It's totally normal to have an emotional spillover sometimes."

"Does it happen to you?"

Faith hesitated before she answered. She didn't break into sobs, the way Stephanie had, but that didn't mean she didn't deal with her own emotional boil-overs from time to time. The only difference was that hers looked different. She didn't cry—she got mad. Or worse, she closed down. "It does," she said finally. "In fact, can I show you something?"

Stephanie nodded and blew her nose once more before Faith led her outside into the warm summer morning.

They didn't speak during the short walk through the trees at the far edge of the yard. In fact, they didn't say a word until Faith led the other woman to a small clearing by the river. It wasn't the little island that was her special spot with Hope growing up, but a different spot. It was only accessible by one path because a large rock outcropping blocked access from any other way. Through the thick trees was a small grassy area just large enough to sit and pick the daisies that grew at the end of summer, listen to the river run over the rocks, and let all your worries drift away. It was where Faith had always come to think and be alone.

It wasn't until both women were sitting in silence for a few minutes, doing just that, before Stephanie finally spoke again. "Thank you." Her voice was barely more than a whisper. "Sometimes I feel really alone," she continued. "It's a strange feeling to be surrounded by people, but still be alone." She crossed her arms over her bent knees and lowered her head to rest. "It's strange, because I know that I don't really know you very well, Faith. But in only a few days, you, Logan, and your friends have made me feel more at home in Glacier Falls than anywhere I've ever been." She looked at Faith then. "And that includes my own hometown." Her smile was tentative. "Thank you for this. I really needed it. And thank you for being a friend."

Friend.

Was that what she was? Faith liked Stephanie. She also felt a profound sense of sadness for the woman. Never before had she met anyone who had so much, but also seemed to have so little.

"You don't need to thank me, Stephanie. It's been really nice getting to know you. And I want you to know that you're welcome to stay in Glacier Falls as long as you want." Faith meant what she said.

"Thank you." She looked as though she might cry again. But this time she was smiling. "You have no idea how much that means. I don't really have a lot of friends, Faith. And... well, I was talking to Dax last night, and we had a thought. Well, I guess I had a thought."

Faith tipped her head and looked at the other woman. Something in her voice told her she might not like what Steph was about to say.

"Everyone here in Glacier Falls has been so welcoming and lovely, Dax and I have decided to have a really small, private wedding ceremony right away instead of the big traditional wedding in a few months. Can we make that happen?"

No big wedding. No big press for Ever After. Small private ceremony.

Everything they'd been doing to get the wedding of the century would be for naught.

The bet.

Her...Logan...

Faith swallowed hard. Stephanie looked so happy, so hopeful. There was only one response.

"Of course." She smiled. "We can make anything happen. Especially if you're okay with a middle of the week wedding. But what do you mean by right away?"

Stephanie bit her bottom lip and giggled. "Thursday?"

"As in *next* Thursday? Or *this* Thursday?"

"Um...*this* Thursday."

Faith shook her head and looked to the ground with a sigh. She'd done crazier things. Finally, she looked up into Stephanie's expectant gaze. "No problem."

"Oh, thank you!" Stephanie clapped her hands. "That's perfect. I'll get all of Dax's flight details and we'll go from there, okay? I really just want to do it before the press gets wind of it and turns it into a circus."

Faith nodded. As much as that circus would be good for business, she could completely understand the desire to avoid it.

"And when it's all over, we'll share the pictures and make sure Ever After is mentioned everywhere." Steph pulled her in for a quick hug. "Don't think I don't know how important that is."

She really was a genuinely sweet person. Faith couldn't deny that. How could she not help her with a beautiful wedding?

"Faith?" Stephanie looked at her with unshed tears shining in her eyes. "I'm really glad I saw that article and came to town."

In response, Faith nodded and they fell once again into silence.

Her thoughts drifted to Logan and their bet that had brought Stephanie to town in the first place.

The bet.

That's all it was: a bet. It wasn't anything more. She needed to remember that because it was so damn hard to keep that clarity when he kissed her. Or touched her. Or put his hands on her. Or…

A bet.

It was just a bet.

Faith glanced at Stephanie and guilt filled her. It was her stupid bet that had brought Stephanie to town, sure. But it was more than that keeping her here, and it would be selfish and hurtful to tell her the truth now. At least not yet.

She reached across, smiled and took her new friend's hand. "I'm really glad, too."

Chapter Ten

"FINALLY!"

When they returned to the house and Faith saw her twin sister at the kitchen table, she burst through the door and raced across the room to pull Hope into a tight hug. "Oh my God, I feel like it's been forever since I've seen you."

Hope laughed, but squeezed her sister even harder in return. "It's only been a few months."

"Might as well have been forever." Faith jumped back. "I'm sorry. I shouldn't squeeze you so hard."

"I'm not going to break."

"You might. The doctors sent you home."

Hope's smile dipped at Faith's concern. "They didn't send me home. We just decided it was for the best."

"That's right," Levi said from the fridge, where he was pulling out a jug of orange juice. "As much as I want to show Hope the world, there's no way I'm doing it at the expense of her health or that of our little miracle there." He winked, and despite the fact that it was super cheesy, Faith couldn't help but feel extra love toward her brother-in-law.

"Besides, it's no fun to see the world from a wheelchair

because I'm not allowed to walk around and raise my blood pressure."

Faith pulled up a chair and sat closer to her sister. "Well, I promise not to do anything to raise your blood pressure now that you're home."

Logan, who was flipping pancakes, snorted with a laugh, and Hope didn't bother hiding her grin. "Whatever you say." She held out her arms for another hug. "I am glad to see you, though. Being home will be so fun." Her gaze flicked over Faith's shoulder for a moment before her eyes twinkled with mischief. "And now that you and Logan have finally decided to get over yourself and…"

Faith shot a warning look at her sister, who summarily ignored her.

"You're together at last," Hope effused. "There's nothing I love more than love."

Faith had to take a deep breath and hold herself back from strangling her sister, who was clearly putting on a first-class show for their guest—whom she'd completely forgotten about for the moment.

She pasted on her biggest, toothiest smile and turned around to wave Stephanie over. "Steph, come meet my sister, Hope. She's as big of a fan of love as you are." Faith turned again and mouthed the words to her sister, "I'm going to kill you later."

Hope only laughed and held out her arms for Stephanie Starz, who gave her a big hug, as if they were long-lost friends.

"I feel like I already know you," Steph said. "Everyone here has been so lovely."

"Yes," Hope said. "Faith is definitely full of the spirit of love these days."

Yup, Faith was going to straight up kill her sister as soon as they were alone.

"And that's why I've decided to have the wedding right

away." Stephanie blurted it out before Faith could even try to break the news that she'd once again taken on a rush wedding. It was starting to become her unintended specialty. "Faith said that as soon as Dax gets here on Wednesday, we can do the ceremony—"

"This Wednesday?" Logan turned around from his cooking at the stove and raised his eyebrows. "Is that right?"

"We don't have anything on Thursday, so…" Faith shrugged. There was nothing she could say.

"Well, if anyone can pull it off, it's my sister." Hope grinned and shook her head before turning back to Stephanie. "Now tell me all about Dax and your wedding."

She left the two ladies to get to know each other a little and went to help Logan with the pancakes.

"Another super-fast wedding?" He raised an eyebrow as she got near. "You really are a glutton for punishment."

That statement could be interpreted so many ways when it came to Logan. Faith opted to ignore him and change the subject. "The pancakes smell great," she told him honestly. He really was an amazing chef. He'd only been staying there for a few days, and she was already sure her pants were fitting a little tighter.

"I made them with love." Logan couldn't even get the words out with a straight face before he was laughing, too.

Everyone was a comedian.

She shook her head, but before she could leave, Logan stuck a small piece of pancake in her mouth. Light, fluffy, and perfect. She nodded with a smile. "Yum. It's—"

"Missing sugar."

"Sugar?"

Logan pressed his lips to hers, wrapped an arm around her waist and dipped her low, right there in the kitchen in front of everyone, which, she realized belatedly, was the point.

"That's exactly what I'm talking about," she heard her

sister say as Logan set her up on her feet again. "They're both fully possessed by the spirit of love."

Faith swallowed back her groan, satisfied that her family was having enough fun for everyone at her expense. "Let's eat."

———

"This really is delicious." Stephanie had filled her plate with her second helping of pancakes, topping them with a healthy dose of maple syrup.

Logan couldn't help but be impressed with her appetite and he didn't bother to hide his look of surprise.

Catching the way he was looking at her, Stephanie laughed. "I'm sorry." She blushed. "I know I'm making a pig of myself, but it's really that good. I can't remember the last time I had homemade pancakes. Or really, pancakes at all. And a home-cooked meal? Well, that was even longer."

"It's okay." Logan waved his fork. "I'm just glad you're enjoying it. And if it's home cooked you're looking for, we should have you over to the Langdon ranch for a proper roast beef dinner. My mom makes an absolutely perfect Yorkshire pudding."

Her eyes lit up with genuine excitement. "Really? I would love that." As soon as the words came out of her mouth, her smile fell from her face. "Sorry. I don't mean to come off so eager, but it's just—"

"It's just that you love hanging out with us so much," Faith cut her off. "And we love hanging out with you." Her smile was warm and totally genuine and within seconds, whatever unease Stephanie was feeling seemed to be gone again.

"I'm so glad because I really can't remember the last time I've enjoyed myself so much. Honestly. I know it must seem so crazy."

"It does," Levi said. "I mean, you must have been all over the world."

Stephanie nodded.

"And seen so much."

She nodded again.

"And the celebrities you must hang out with," Hope added.

Stephanie only shrugged. "But it's not..." She waved her arms around the table. "This."

"You think this is special?" It was Hope who asked, but there was nothing sarcastic in her question.

"I do. Very special." Stephanie lowered her head a little and shook it before looking up with a shrug. "I mean, I know this is going to sound pretty stupid, but I'm actually really jealous of you all. I was an only child, and you had your sister."

Faith and Hope automatically flashed identical smiles as they looked at each other.

"And Logan and Levi? You guys had each other and all of you...well, you grew up together."

"We did." Faith rolled her eyes. "And trust me," she shot a look at Logan that he was sure was supposed to be sarcastic, but all he felt was a flash of desire deep in his gut, "it wasn't always as awesome as you think it was."

Stephanie laughed. "I'm sure it wasn't. But what I wouldn't have given to experience a little bit of that myself."

She looked so wistful and innocent, that, for a moment, Logan completely forgot that she was quite literally a mega celebrity sitting in their kitchen, chatting with them all as if she were just a regular person.

"Well then, you should." The words were out of Logan's mouth before he'd actually registered what they meant.

Everyone at the table turned to look at him with questions in their eyes.

It was Levi who picked up the ball and ran with it. "Yes,"

he said with a slap on the table that rattled the glasses. "Why don't you move in here until the wedding?"

"What?"

"What?"

Both Logan and Faith asked at the same time. Logan hadn't been sure what he'd meant when he'd said what he'd said, but it definitely wasn't that. After all, they were totally lying to the poor woman, and having her under the same roof would surely only make that a million times harder. Beneath the table, Faith punched him in the thigh.

"What the—" He spun to face her, but the words fell from his tongue as he saw the look she was giving him. A look that said very clearly that having Stephanie Starz move in with them was the worst possible thing that could happen, and it was all his fault.

Maybe it was.

She was going to kill him.

But...

"Absolutely." Logan ignored the way Faith's hand squeezed his thigh in a vise grip. "It's only for a few days, really. Maybe she could use the baby's room?" He looked directly at Hope. "After all, it's only for a little bit, and you still have plenty of time to get it ready."

Logan was well aware that he'd used an argument directly in opposition to what he had said in order to convince Faith to let him move in to her room, but it was just a means to an end. Because if Stephanie stayed in the spare room that would one day become the baby's room, then there was no way he'd be able to stay on the couch again, which meant...

Still ignoring the increasing pressure Faith was putting on his leg, he slipped his own hand across to her thigh and squeezed gently.

He was going to be once again in her bed, a place he very

much liked to be. And now there wasn't a damn thing she could do about it.

Not that he thought even for a minute that she wanted to.

She put on a good show, but Logan wasn't a fool. He knew damn well that she wanted him there just as much as he wanted to be there.

Now, all he needed to do was get her to admit it.

He gave her a final squeeze of her thigh, to which she responded with a hard pinch of his. "Ow! Dammit!" All eyes turned to him, so Logan did his best to grin as he caught Faith's hand in his own under the table and held it tight to prevent it from doing more damage. "I just realized all the work I need to get to today," he said as a pathetic cover. "That barn isn't going to clean itself after last night's wedding. It was a good one, wasn't it?"

Faith glared at him, but begrudgingly nodded. "It was a tricky one, but it turned out perfectly."

"They're all a little tricky in their own way, aren't they?" Hope's face lit up, talking about weddings again. She really was a true romantic. She absolutely loved this stuff. "But don't you find them all just so…" Her hands fluttered to her chest. "Romantic."

Faith groaned a little but she smiled. "Truthfully? I think I do."

Hope turned to their guest and started to explain. "You have to understand, Stephanie. My sister here wasn't always a believer in love."

"Really?"

"Really." They all nodded, including Faith, who shrugged as Hope continued. "In fact, when we were younger, she was completely against the whole concept of love or marriage or any of it. It was crazy. I never could understand it."

Logan kept his eyes on Faith, whose face had completely

shifted while her sister was speaking. Her mouth was pressed into a line and her eyebrows furrowed with...*worry?*

"It wasn't until this summer that she finally realized what she's been missing." Hope beamed at her sister. "And finally came to her senses with Logan."

Under the table, he squeezed her hand in support—and maybe a bit of comradery.

"That's so crazy." Steph speared a piece of melon on her plate and brought it to her mouth. "But it only makes your story even more romantic and special. Don't you think?"

Faith hesitated before answering. She swallowed hard but couldn't seem to find the words, so Logan jumped in.

"I think that a little Irish cream in this coffee would make it absolutely perfect." He released Faith's hand and pushed up from the table. "Anyone else? We keep it up here, right?" He moved across the kitchen to the cupboard over the fridge, where he knew the women kept their alcohol.

"If we have any, it should be—"

"Got it." Logan pulled the bottle out. A manila envelope fell out to the floor as he did so. "What's this?"

Faith was up and across the room before he could even straighten up again. She snatched it from his hand and folded it in half. "It's mine. Don't worry about it."

"Is it important?" Hope moved to push her chair back, but Levi held her in place with a hand on her shoulder and a concerned look.

"It's not." Faith moved quickly and shoved the envelope into her purse, but not before Logan noticed the panicked look on her face. When she turned around again, she faced the room with a smile. "Now, where's that Irish cream, Logan? I think we could all use some. Except you, Hope."

Chapter Eleven

BRUNCH COULDN'T END SOON ENOUGH, AS far as Faith was concerned. Of course it dragged on and on, before finally Stephanie excused herself to go check out of her hotel and prepare herself to move into their house.

The whole idea of Stephanie Starz living in her house made Faith's head hurt, but she couldn't let herself think about the details of that particular problem at the moment. What she really needed to do was spend some time with her sister. First, she needed to deal with one thing.

Faith waited until Logan and Levi headed out toward the barn. Levi had offered to help out so she could visit with Hope, who'd relocated upstairs to her bedroom. She looked out the kitchen window and as soon as they reached the barn door, she grabbed her purse—and the envelope inside—and sprinted upstairs to her room.

She stood in the doorway and looked around. *Where could she hide it?*

She'd completely forgotten that she'd stuffed the envelope in the kitchen cabinet weeks ago. Thank goodness no one had found it before. It's not that she liked keeping secrets, or even that she wanted to. In fact, she'd been about to show Hope exactly what was in there when Hope told her that she was having trouble with her pregnancy and was supposed to avoid stress of all kinds. How the hell could she tell her then the very thing that would be guaranteed to stress out her sister? It was definitely a secret she needed to know, but now was not the time. She'd waited all these years; she could wait a little longer.

Which was why she needed to hide the envelope. In the dresser? No. Logan had a drawer in her dresser now; he could open the wrong one and find it.

The closet?

Same problem.

Damn. Logan. He was everywhere all of a sudden.

If she hadn't already been so worked up, Faith might have taken a minute to acknowledge the vibrations that ran through her body at the thought of him. Vibrations that went straight to that spot low in her belly and caused her mind to travel to all kinds of dirty locations the second she looked at the bed where together, they'd—

"Whatcha doing?"

Faith whirled around to see her sister in the doorway. Belatedly, she realized she was clutching the envelope in her hands.

Hope laughed. "I don't know what I should ask you about first. The envelope or that blush on your face." She nodded toward the bed. "I think we have a lot to talk about, sis."

Shit. Shit. Shit.

Faith contemplated lying, but no one in the world knew her better than her twin sister. There was no point in lying or trying to cover anything up. But she might have a chance at distracting her. "I thought you were supposed to be in bed." She gave Hope her best chastising look and walked toward her, with a shooing motion. "Come on. I'll come into your room. We can talk and you can ask me anything you want."

"Anything?"

Faith shrugged. "Doesn't mean I'll answer."

A few minutes later, Hope was settled into the bed and Faith had safely stashed the envelope under the mattress on her side of the bed. It wasn't ideal, but she'd find a better location for it later.

She hopped up on her sister's bed and grabbed an extra pillow to hug into her lap. "I'm glad you're home."

Hope smiled. "I'm glad too, but a little sad." Her smile dipped. "This was supposed to be our big adventure."

"I think becoming a mom will be a big enough adventure, don't you?"

"I think so." Hope laughed. "And speaking of big adventures..." She wiggled her eyebrows but Faith rolled her eyes and shrugged.

"No adventures here, I'm afraid. I've been working like a slave and that's all I've had time for."

"Bullshit."

She should have known better. As much as she'd been excited to see Hope, she'd also known that her sister was going to be able to see right through her. It was annoying, to be sure.

"Because," Hope continued, "that bite mark on your neck tells me you've been having at least a certain kind of adventure."

"What?" Her hand flew to her neck. "I don't have a bite mark!" She slipped off the bed and ran into Hope's attached bathroom while she spoke. "I'm not a teenager. I don't have—"

Shit.

"What were you saying?" Hope sounded as though she was only barely containing her laughter as Faith continued to stare at her reflection in the mirror.

It was true. How had she not seen it before? She had a hickey on her neck, just below her ear. It wasn't hugely obvious, but clearly her sister had seen it. Which meant...

How unprofessional!

Had she worn her hair up at the wedding yesterday? Of course she had. She always wore it up in a twist to keep it out of her way while she was working. Which meant that every single person who she'd engaged with had seen the evidence of her...

Ugh.

"I've already seen it, Faith. Don't even bother trying to hide it." Her sister sounded downright cheerful.

"Glad I could entertain you," she said as she returned from the bathroom and sat on the bed again.

"But what I really want are the details on how it got there."

"What?"

"Okay, okay." Hope laughed. "Maybe not all the details." She made a show of hiding her eyes and shaking her head. "But I do want to know what changed so dramatically while I was gone. Because...this..." She waved her hand around. "Is definitely a change. You swore upside down and sideways that you were never going to have a relationship with Logan Langdon."

"Whoa. This is *not* a relationship."

Wasn't it?

Faith shook her head violently. "He bet me that I couldn't pull off the loved-up act to give Stephanie Starz what she wanted in a fairy-tale romance story for Ever After Ranch. I took the bet. If I win, he leaves me alone."

Hope's eyes twinkled with mischief. "And if he wins?"

If I win, you spend a night with me.

Faith could remember Logan's words exactly. And more importantly, the exact way he looked at her, with heat in his eyes when he gave her his terms. The thing was, she'd already spent the night with him. Did that mean he'd won?

No.

He definitely hadn't won.

Not yet.

Not ever!

"It's not important." She shook her head. "He won't."

"Well, it looks to me like there's a bit more than a bet going on here." Hope reached for her sister's hair that was trying and failing to cover the love bite on her neck. "Don't tell me that sleeping together was all part of the elaborate lie." Her face shifted briefly. "Which, by the way, I'm not totally on board with. Stephanie seems like a total sweetheart and you know how I feel about lying."

"I know. I know. I hate it too. It just kind of escalated. We'll tell her the truth." It was a decision she'd just made, but it felt right.

Hope dipped her head and rolled her shoulders before looking up again. "Do you think we should?"

"What?" Her sister was the *good* one. Hope didn't lie. It wasn't her style. Faith had known she would be upset about the whole thing with Stephanie. She'd expected it. She hadn't expected this. "You don't think we should tell her?"

"Well...do you think sometimes it's kinder not to tell the truth?"

Faith sat back and gave her head a shake. "What are you talking about?"

"Clearly, she's kind of a lost soul. I get the impression that she doesn't have a lot of friends and she just seems...lonely." Her sister shrugged. "I guess I don't see the harm in keeping up the act for a little bit if it gives her a good experience. I mean, it's not really a *total* lie." She wiggled her eyebrows. "You two clearly have something going on."

Faith had to hold back the urge to toss a pillow at her sister. Despite the fact that it was true. She had something going on with Logan, although for the life of her, she had no idea what it was. Not really. Never in her life had she been so conflicted. Especially over a man. Whenever he was near, her entire body went on full alert in anticipation of what would happen next.

And what she *wanted* to happen next. Because despite her protests, and what her *brain* might want from Logan, it was *very* different from what her *body* wanted.

More and more, she couldn't be sure of what her *heart* wanted. And that was the whole problem.

"Hello?" Hope waved her hand in front of her face. "Earth to Faith. I was just saying how maybe we should go easy with Stephanie for a few more days and show her a good time."

Faith nodded. "I agree."

She didn't bother mentioning how doing so would mean that Logan would be once again in her bed, because then she might have to admit that she *wanted* him in her bed.

And what was so wrong with that?

"Seriously, Faith. I feel like even though you're sitting here, you're a million miles away. What is going on? Is this about Logan?"

Of course it was. But she couldn't say that to her sister. She couldn't tell her twin, whom she'd always told everything to, that despite spending a lifetime railing against the idea of love or falling for anyone, she might actually—

"You're falling for him."

What the—

Faith blinked hard and stared at her twin.

"You are," Hope said with a self-assured nod. "You totally are. And what's so wrong with that?"

"It's not...I'm not...what are you even talking about?"

Hope crossed her arms, looking very sure of herself. "What are *you* talking about?" She chuckled. "There's nothing wrong with falling in love, Faith. In fact, it's pretty freaking awesome. I never did understand your whole aversion to it."

Right. Faith's thoughts shot back to the envelope she'd just hidden in her room. That envelope contained the secrets of why she'd never let herself believe in love. Hope and Faith had grown up with the perfect parents. They were loving and supportive and more importantly, they loved each other more than anything in the world. At least, that's what they told the world. But the day that Faith had come down the stairs and heard them arguing, saying terrible things to each other, the image of their perfection had changed for her. She'd been fifteen when she'd discovered that loving someone, and letting them love you in return, meant that they would have the power to destroy you with only a few words.

No thank-you.

"Talk to me, Faith." Hope's voice had shifted. Her eyes were full of worry as she reached for her sister's hand. "Tell me why you've spent so long fighting this. What was so terrible that you turned your back for so long?"

The urge to confide in her sister was so strong it was almost a physical ache. But at the same time, she'd always protected Hope. The truth would hurt, and what was the point of that?

Still…

Faith took a deep breath. "I don't know, Hope. You're not supposed to be stressed about anything and—"

"Not knowing is stressing me out. Now, spill."

Faith couldn't help but smile at her sister's stubbornness. She also knew it was probably true. No doubt Hope would work herself up if she didn't tell her the truth. Besides, it was time. She was tired of carrying secrets.

"Wait here."

As soon as the decision was made, it was like a weight she didn't know she was carrying was lifted from her shoulders. Faith quickly retrieved the envelope from where she'd stashed it only minutes earlier and returned to Hope's bed.

Once she showed it to her sister, there would be no going back. She could never take it back and the truth would finally be out in the open. Faith couldn't decide whether that was a good or bad thing.

She took a deep breath. "Are you sure you want to know?"

Hope hesitated, obviously sensing the gravity of what her sister was about to show her. But just as Faith knew she would, she nodded and Faith handed her the envelope.

Cleaning up after an event with a helper who knew what they were doing made everything exceptionally easier. Especially when that helper wasn't the woman you wanted to pin up against the wall and kiss senseless until she begged for more.

Logan looked over at his cousin.

Yes. Working without all the sexual tension was definitely easier. But not nearly as much fun.

"Why are you looking at me that way?" Levi tossed a tablecloth into the pile and searched for another one. "It's creeping me out."

Logan chuckled. "I was just trying to decide if it was a good thing that you're not Faith."

Levi shook his head and tossed another tablecloth in the pile. "That may be the strangest thing you've ever said to me." He tipped his head to the side. "Well, maybe not *the* strangest thing. But still, what the hell?"

"Well, on one hand, we can burn through this so much faster if I'm not looking at you wondering how I can get you naked in the next thirty seconds." He ignored Levi's exaggerated shocked expression. "But on the other hand," Logan continued, "it would be a lot more fun if I was."

"Wondering how to get me naked?" Levi tugged at the hem of his T-shirt. "Here, want me to—"

"Oh, hell no." Logan tossed a pile of dirty napkins in his direction and laughed. "To clarify, it would be a lot more fun if you were Faith, and I was trying to figure out how to get you naked."

"Right." Levi laughed. "What is going on with the two of you, anyway? Obviously there's some nakedness."

"Some," Logan agreed. "But…" He drifted off. Levi was his best friend and if he was going to confide in anyone, it would be him, but somehow it didn't feel right giving him the private details. The last thing he wanted to do was lessen what had happened between him and Faith the other night. If anything, he wanted to make sure it happened again. And he might not know much, but he knew enough to know that it would never happen again if he wasn't careful.

Levi waited a minute, but when Logan didn't continue, he shook his head and went back to clearing the tables. "Whatever, man. All I'm going to say is it's about time the two of you got over each other and got together."

"You know we're not actually together, right?"

Levi shook his head. "Whatever you say."

"But damn it, I'd like to be." It came out of his mouth so quickly, Logan didn't even realize what he'd said.

Not until Levi ran across the barn floor and slapped him on the back. "You what?"

Logan shook his head and looked at his cousin, realizing what he'd just said out loud. And more importantly, how much he'd meant it. He'd always been attracted to Faith. Ever since they were kids, he got a knot in his gut when she was around. But she'd obviously never felt the same. At least, she sure acted like she didn't. There'd been a few times he'd thought maybe, just maybe he'd caught her looking at him with that look in her eyes, but as soon as he tried to make a move, she shot him down. Repeatedly.

Sure, he'd been a kid with absolutely zero game, but his instincts couldn't have been that far off. And a young man could only handle so much rejection before he started to take it personally. So it had become a game instead. How many ways could he make Faith Turner blush? Or smack him? Or roll her eyes? Or get really angry? That was the big payoff. If he could cross the line enough to piss her off, then he knew how much she cared.

Yes, he'd been a stupid teenage boy, who'd clearly gotten it backward. But some attention was better than none, right?

Wrong.

Those days were over. Now that he'd had a little taste of it, he wanted all the attention. All of the *right* kind of attention. He shook his head and told Levi as much.

"You're in trouble then, my friend." Levi shook his head. "I'm not sure Faith Turner is capable of the right kind of attention. I mean, she's never really been the type."

It was true and exactly what he'd been thinking, but he didn't need to hear it. Especially because it was the last thing he wanted to believe. Logan shrugged off his cousin's opinion.

"Well, there's nothing I like more than a challenge, is there?"

Levi shook his head and let out a low whistle. "There are challenges, and there is Faith. Challenge doesn't even begin to explain how hardheaded she can be. Especially when it comes to you."

Logan let a smile cross his face and Levi laughed. "Something tells me this is going to get interesting."

It was going to get interesting, all right, because it wasn't just a game anymore. Maybe it never had been. He'd spent way too long chasing Faith; it was time she knew exactly how he felt about her because those feelings were not going away. Not anytime soon.

When he was finished up in the barn and Levi left to run errands for Hope, Logan locked up and hopped in his truck. He'd been so busy with Ever After Ranch planning weddings and helping Faith with…well, everything…he'd been completely slacking in regards to his duties at the Langdon ranch for the last few months. He felt bad about it, especially considering this was his mother's first summer since his father had passed away. Dad had always handled the running of things—with Logan's help, of course—and Levi's help, too, when they were younger, before Levi had run off.

When he was younger, Logan had always expected that he'd take over the ranch and his father would retire. Maybe his parents could finally travel together and see the world. After all, they'd worked so hard their entire life, they deserved a little down time. But Harold had never wanted to let go. It was almost as if the harder Logan pushed him to give up some of the duties, the more he resisted. Over time, Logan had even begun to lose interest in the ranch he'd grown up on, which was why when Hope and Levi asked him whether he'd be willing to help out Faith with Ever After, he'd jumped at it.

Well, maybe working closely with Faith had something to do with it, too. Still, he'd enjoyed the change of pace.

But it didn't make him feel any less guilty when it came to leaving his mom in charge.

Logan drove through the gates and into the yard. He parked the truck out in front of the house, but something told him to walk out behind the barn to find his mom.

Sure enough, Debbie was leaning on the wooden fence, one booted foot on the bottom rung, her arms crossed to rest her head as she watched the activity in the horse ring.

"Hey, Mom."

As if Debbie had expected him, she didn't stand, but turned her head in greeting, a smile on her face. "To what do I owe this pleasure? Don't tell me Faith kicked you out already?"

Logan laughed. "I'm sure she would if she could." He leaned on the fence next to her. "New colt?"

Inside the ring, Travis, one of the ranch hands Debbie had hired was walking with a young horse, leading it with a rope.

Debbie nodded. "But not one of ours. Travis asked me if he could use the stables and since we really don't have many horses of our own anymore, I thought…"

Logan nodded. Travis was one of the ranch hands his mom had hired. Logan didn't know him well, but he seemed like a good guy and a hard worker. He raised a hand in greeting as the other man looked over.

"You seem kind of sad, Mom. What's going on?"

"Not sad," Debbie answered. "Just thoughtful."

She'd gone back to watching the horse, so Logan couldn't see her face.

"I'm really sorry I haven't been around, Mom. I feel like I should—"

"Nonsense." She stood up straight finally and looked at him.

Maybe it was his imagination, but his mother seemed to have aged since he last saw her only a few days ago.

"Don't you feel bad for a second. This ranch isn't your responsibility. It's mine. I don't expect you to put your life on hold so I can keep doing…" She shook her head. "Doing whatever it is that I'm doing." Her voice fell and she dropped her gaze. "And frankly, Logan, I don't know what it is that I'm doing anymore."

"Mom?" Concern filled him. He'd never heard his mother speak this way. He took her hand and led her to a picnic table nearby where they could sit. "What's going on?"

It took her a moment to answer him, but finally she spoke. "I'm going to sell the ranch."

Whatever Logan had been expecting, it hadn't been that. "What? You're going to do what?"

"It's time, Logan."

"How is it time?"

She couldn't sell the ranch. It was his home. It was where he worked. What he did.

It was what you used to do.

Too agitated to sit, Logan jumped up and paced. "But if you sell it, what will I do?"

It was incredibly selfish and he knew it, but he couldn't seem to stop himself from asking the question.

"You'll figure something out," she answered calmly. "You seem to like working with Faith at Ever After, and I'm sure—"

"But what will you do?"

It was the better question, and he was more than a little disappointed he hadn't asked it first.

Her face split into a broad smile. "Travel," she said simply. "I've always wanted to see the world and hearing about some of the places Hope and Levi had been, well, it just made it all the more real for me."

"Travel?"

Debbie nodded. "As much as I can. Your father never wanted to go anywhere, and as much as I miss him, I think it's also time for me to live my own life."

He couldn't argue with that.

"And you and Katie are both moving on and have different interests now. It's not fair to saddle you with something you don't even want."

Did he *want* the ranch? He didn't even have to think about it. As much as he'd loved growing up there, and all the memories they had, he didn't want to be a rancher. It wasn't the lifestyle for him.

"Katie said she had a bunch of ideas about things. Have you spoken to her?" His sister had just finished taking her degree in business online, and throughout the whole process was compiling a list of ideas to improve the running of the ranch and their operations. Now that he was thinking about it, Katie had never shared that list with them.

"No." Debbie shook her head. "And now she has her own business to concern herself with. Besides, it wouldn't matter. I've made up my mind."

Logan sat again and stared at the wooden plank of the picnic table. It needed to be sanded and stained. In fact, most of the things on the ranch needed some upkeep. And he sure as hell didn't feel like doing any of it.

He nodded and they sat in silence for a few minutes. Finally, he asked, "Does Katie know?"

"Not yet." His mom reached over and took his hand. "You okay with all this?"

Logan didn't hesitate. He stood, walked around the table, and pulled his mom into a big hug. "I just want you to be happy, Mom."

"That's my line." She laughed. "And speaking of being happy, how are things going with Faith?"

Chapter Twelve

IT DIDN'T TAKE LONG for Stephanie to pack her few bags into the back of her rented SUV and check out of the Big Rock Inn. It had been a comfortable hotel, and despite the fact that it was nothing like the five-star spa resorts she was used to staying at, the small-town charm of the Big Rock Inn might have been her favorite accommodation in a long time. Nothing prestigious or arrogant about it. Just quality comfort.

Still, Stephanie was looking forward to moving out of the small space, to move into the Turners' household for a few days. She probably should have felt weird about moving in with virtual strangers, but she didn't. Not even a little bit. From the moment she'd met Faith and then Hope—maybe even from the moment she'd seen the article online—she'd felt a connection to them.

It was hard to explain, or maybe even impossible, but she felt as though she'd known the sisters and their partners all her life. As if they were family. No doubt, Dax would think she was crazy. And Terri, her assistant, would lose her mind if she knew where she was going to stay. Terri was beyond protective and cautious.

And maybe she was crazy. But it sure didn't feel that way. It felt right. Even if it was only for a few days, she could pretend to be part of a family. A big, loud, loving family. Like she never had.

But she couldn't show up empty-handed. She needed to take something. Like a hostess gift. Something appropriate. But what?

Stephanie gazed down the main street and took it all in. Glacier Falls really was the perfect small mountain town. A variety of shops lined the street, each with large baskets of flowers out front and trees on the boulevard that made you feel as if you were in the middle of a Hallmark movie. People everywhere waved and stopped to say hello, and not once had she been treated the way she was in Hollywood. Sure, people had asked for her autograph, which she'd happily given out along with selfies, but no one had hounded her, or hunted her the way the paparazzi did in California. It had been a refreshing break, and more than a little eye-opening. There were other places to live. Maybe she didn't need to be in the thick of the craziness anymore. Maybe she could finally choose where she wanted to be.

She wasn't the only one choosing to leave the chaos of Hollywood behind, either. Cal McCormick, another major movie star who'd made his fame in Australia, had moved a few years ago to a town called Cedar Springs that was only about an hour away from where she was now. Sure, the show he was starring in was filmed there, but it was also where his entire family was, and his partner, Milena. But still, if he could do it, why couldn't she?

Stephanie couldn't wait to show Dax Glacier Falls so he could fall in love with the town, the same way. *Soon,* she reminded herself. *As soon as he was done with his shoot.* And one of the first things she was going to show him was the bakery, Sweetie Pies, and their famous honey buns. Her eyes landed on the bakery, but it was her nose that picked up the delicious scent first.

Honey buns would be a perfect gift to take the Turners. From what she'd seen, no one could resist them.

A few minutes later, after chatting with the bakery owner for a few minutes, she had a box wrapped in string and full of the delicious treats in one hand and a chai latte in the other. She still wasn't in a rush to head over to Ever After; she didn't want to look too eager, after all, so she found a little table on the sidewalk patio and settled in to people watch.

It didn't take long, of course, for her to attract attention, but she didn't mind, especially when Katie Banks, the owner of the Hub who'd she'd rented the kayak from the other day, approached her with a man she hadn't met.

"Stephanie! It's nice to see you."

"And you." She got up and gave her new friend a quick hug before turning to the man. "I don't think we've met." She extended her hand, which he took in a firm handshake with a warm smile.

"I'm Nick Newton. A friend of Katie's husband, Damon."

He was handsome, with dirty-blonde hair and green eyes and a wicked smile that meant he was trouble. But there was something else about him. Something a little nerdy, in a good way, and she took an instant liking to him. "Nice to meet you, Nick. Are you in town visiting, too?"

"I am." He ran a hand through his hair, leaving it tousled and messy. "Just trying to figure out what to do with my life, ya know?"

"Nick was Damon's business partner once upon a time and now that they've sold, poor Nick here is lost, with no purpose in life," Katie supplied. "I'm trying to convince him to invest in a local business and stay here, but so far…"

"So far I haven't figured anything out." He shrugged. "But

I do like it here." He elbowed Katie good-naturedly. "And the company is pretty good, too."

"Maybe too good." She laughed. "But you know we like having you around." Her smile was genuine. "But on that note, I need to get to the store. Sorry to run, but hopefully I'll see you again soon, Stephanie."

"Call me Steph. And I certainly hope so."

Nick stayed behind as Katie ran off down the street. "Do you mind if I join you for a few minutes? Like Katie said, I really don't have anywhere to be."

Steph patted the seat next to her. She liked Nick and the idea of a little company was nice.

"So, how are you liking Glacier Falls?" Nick asked when he was seated. "Everyone treating you like a normal person here?"

She laughed. "They are. How about you?"

It was his turn to laugh, but he nodded seriously, too. "They are. But I can't say many people know who I am here."

Steph sat up in her chair and looked at him closely. *Was he an actor? Or maybe a recording artist?*

"It's okay," he said when she didn't reply. "Most people outside of the tech world don't know who I am either. And I'm nowhere near your status."

It never failed to make her blush when people referred to how famous she was. She didn't like to think of herself as anything other than a normal person, even though those days were long over.

"So who are you, then?" She was glad to have the attention off her.

He waved away the question. "Just an inventor, really. It's not a big deal."

Steph eyed him carefully and when he didn't offer any more information, she said, "You know I'm just going to get it out of Katie later, so you might as well tell me and save me the trouble."

His eyes flashed with mischief, but he nodded. "That's a good point. And honestly, I'm not trying to be coy about it, but compared to your level of fame, mine is, well…nonexistent." He held up his hands in a shrug. "But here it is. A few years ago, Damon and I were in school together. We dropped out when we designed a microchip and no," he added quickly, "I'm not allowed to say what it was or what it did." He shrugged again. "Confidentiality agreement. Anyway, we sold it for a zillion dollars and…"

"Now you're a rock star in the tech world."

"Pretty much."

They both laughed and Steph took a sip of her latte. "So really, no one would recognize you?"

Nick shook his head dramatically. "Not true. Damon and I were featured in *Tech Time* about a year ago and it was crazy." He flashed a deadly smile. "I'm not going to lie—I kind of liked the attention that being a cover model will get you."

She couldn't help but laugh. He really was charming, in a dorky way. "I bet you did. Were you fighting off the ladies?" She was joking, but the look on his face told her she'd nailed the situation exactly. "Wow. I had no idea the tech world was so…"

"Sexy?"

She rolled her eyes but Nick changed the subject. "So what's your story? I think I heard a rumor that you're in town to—"

"Get married." Saying it out loud made her both excited and nervous at the same time. She'd been so sure of her decision to have a quick and quiet ceremony, but still, she couldn't help the little flicker of doubt that popped up every once in a while.

Nick shook his head and groaned. "Not you, too."

"Me too?"

"All the good ones in this town are getting snapped up and locked down."

It was such a ridiculous thing to say, they both burst out laughing, and it felt good. In fact, Steph couldn't remember the last time she'd been so relaxed and completely at ease. A few minutes later, their conversation had shifted to potential business opportunities in Glacier Falls, and Steph found herself enjoying her time so much, that when her phone rang with the familiar ringtone that would normally make her drop everything, she let it go straight to voice mail.

She'd call Dax later.

Chapter Thirteen

HOPE TOOK the envelope from her and slowly pulled out the papers inside. The same papers that Faith had read over and over since she'd discovered them right after their parents' deaths. Of course, she'd gone looking for them. Hope had never known they'd existed.

Faith waited while Hope read them over. She watched her sister's face carefully as everything registered and the enormity of what she was looking at settled in.

"Adoption?" Hope asked after a moment. "I don't understand. Why would Mom and Dad have a proof of adoption?" Her face transformed in a flash and she sat up in bed. "Wait! We were adopted?"

It was a reasonable question, even if it didn't make any sense at all. The girls were an exact combination of both their mother and father. With their mother's upturned nose, and long blonde hair. They got their blue eyes, big smile and their height from their father. Faith didn't need to say anything before Hope shook her head and looked once again at the papers that really didn't offer much in the way of explanation.

"Help me out here, Faith. What is this?" She held out the

paper that outlined the adoption order as well as the birth registration. "This doesn't make sense."

"I know. It wouldn't have made any sense to me either, if I hadn't overheard them fighting about it." Before her sister could ask any more questions, Faith settled on the bed and started talking. "It was late. We were about fifteen—almost sixteen, maybe—and I heard them arguing. It woke me up because they never argued. Not like this." She closed her eyes and remembered the day she'd snuck down the stairs to see what was going on. They were on the porch, the bright sunny day a direct contrast to the hurtful words they were throwing at each other. "Mom and Dad never saw me. They never knew I was there, and so, I guess, they never knew that I knew the truth."

"Which was?"

"That Mom had a baby before us."

Hope's eyes grew wide.

"Before she'd even met Dad, I guess. I don't know the details." Faith shrugged. "But the way I heard it, Mom hadn't told Dad about it. Ever."

Hope shook her head. "No way. They knew everything about each other. They were perfect together. They were the—"

"The perfect couple," Faith supplied for her with a groan. That had been the entire problem when she was young. They had been the very image of blissful love. Everyone had thought so—including the twins. That is, until Faith had witnessed the fight.

"They were saying terrible things to each other, Hope." Faith finally told her everything she'd held in for so long in an effort to protect her sister. "He called her a slut and a—well... worse. And she told him that she hated him. People who love each other don't talk that way."

"Couples fight, Faith."

She shook her head with the memory. "But to say things like that? No. That's beyond fighting. How do you ever come back from that? You can't, Hope. For the rest of their lives, they pretended everything was fine and they were still madly in love. As if they hadn't ripped each other's hearts out. If that's love…forget it."

Hope watched her with sadness in her eyes. "That's not how it works, Faith. You know better than that. You know they would have fought and made up. You just didn't see that part. You can't possibly think that they were pretending the whole time?"

She shrugged and Hope groaned.

"You didn't?"

"Okay, I mean… I guess logically I must have known that they would have… It doesn't matter now," she interrupted her sister. "All that matters is now you know the truth. No more secrets."

Faith pulled her sister into a tight hug. "It's so good to have you back, Hope." Her words were muffled by her sister's shoulder, and her own tears that had surprised her, but she didn't bother trying to wipe them away.

"It's so good to be back." Hope kissed her on the cheek and sat up. She grabbed up the papers previously abandoned next to her and waved them in the space between them. "Now… what are we going to do about this? I can't believe you kept this from me for all this time. We have a sister, Faith. A sister!"

Faith sat back and took a deep breath. She'd just revealed to her twin, whom she always told everything to, that she had kept the biggest secret of their lives from her, and instead of Hope being mad, she was…excited? She looked at her sister in question. "You're not super pissed at me for not telling you?"

"Of course I am!" Hope smacked her on the arm. "But what's the point of that? Right now, we have more important things to worry about." She waved the papers again. "Like finding our sister."

Faith shook her head in wonder, although she shouldn't be surprised. Hope's capacity to love and forgive was what made her so great, and as far as Faith was concerned, the better twin. "How do you propose you're going to do that?"

The papers didn't have much information at all. It was only a birth record, with no name, just the time and place of the baby's birth, and the sex. Accompanied by a letter from the adoption agency, that there was nothing more they could reveal.

"It looks like Mom wrote for information when the baby would have been eighteen," Hope said, rereading the letter.

"Right, but that's not much to go on." Faith couldn't even begin to imagine where to start with such a project. It seemed completely overwhelming. "It will take ages to figure it out."

"Well, it's a good thing I've got ages." Hope grinned. "After all, what else am I supposed to do while I'm on bed rest?" She laughed. "It'll give me something to do. Besides, I've always wanted to play detective. This could be a lot of fun."

Faith couldn't help but laugh, too. Telling her sister the truth after all this time had been more of a relief than she could have even known. "Maybe it will be fun. For you," she added quickly. "I'll run the business, and you figure out who our sister is. Deal?"

"Absolutely!" Hope stuck out her hand to shake and when Faith took it, she added, "Besides, I wouldn't want to get in the way of you figuring out your real feelings for Logan."

Faith's mouth dropped open and she tried to pull away, but Hope held her fast.

"Don't pretend you don't know something real is going on there. I, for one, am totally over it. It's ridiculous and you know it."

Faith opened her mouth to say something, but her sister cut

her off again. "It is. I know you well enough to know the truth. But I also know you well enough to know you'll figure it out." Hope pulled her close and gave her a smooch on the cheek. "Now, can you bring me my laptop? I have work to do."

She did as she asked and when she finally left the room, Faith leaned back against the wall and dropped her head to her chest. Hope thought she knew what was going on, but she didn't. At least not all of it. Maybe there was something real with Logan? But more likely, he was just trying to win the bet. That's the way Logan was. He liked to poke at her and rile her up. And he liked to win.

Hope wasn't too far off the mark when it came to how Faith felt. But Logan? That was a much bigger question, one she certainly couldn't answer. And it was an awful lot to bet her heart on after all this time unless she could know for sure.

How were things going with Faith?

His mother had asked a good question. A *very* good question, and one Logan wanted answers to more than his mother. Who, judging by the way she wouldn't let the subject drop, wanted answers very badly.

But Logan couldn't answer her, if he didn't know himself.

What he did know was that things were about to get a whole lot more cozy now that Stephanie Starz had moved in. She'd arrived at the house, shortly after Logan himself had returned, with a box of honey buns from Sweetie Pies and a huge smile on her face.

It had been an eventful evening, and not just because they had a guest. But right before Stephanie had arrived, Hope and Faith had dropped a bomb on the guys by revealing the secret Faith had been keeping for years about a long-lost adopted sister. Shocked would have been an understatement, but Hope didn't seem upset by the news at all. She was excited and energized to *play detective*, as she put it. They'd decided to not mention anything to Stephanie about it all, considering she had enough to worry about with her wedding coming up so quickly.

In true Levi form, he was supportive of anything his wife wanted, as long as it didn't stress Hope out and put the baby at risk.

Not that Hope would do anything to put her pregnancy at risk.

Logan didn't have much to say about the whole situation. It all seemed so crazy. So he let the others lead the conversation with ideas and strategies about how to go about finding the truth. Instead of contributing, he watched Faith, who was also quieter than usual. Especially considering the topic of conversation. He would have thought she'd have lots to say, but instead, she seemed distant and withdrawn for most of the night. Even once Stephanie arrived, and the conversation changed to weddings, Faith stayed quiet and let Hope lead the conversation. Either no one else noticed, or they'd let it go. But Logan hadn't let it go. And he'd been hoping to ask her about it, if she ever came up to bed. Which was looking less and less likely because he'd been upstairs for almost forty minutes, and she still hadn't come up.

Logan was just about to go looking for her, because he was pretty sure he was the reason she was lingering downstairs, when the door to their now officially shared bedroom opened.

"I thought you might be asleep."

"I thought you might be hoping for that," he answered with a grin. "Disappointed?"

She shrugged, but then surprised him with her honest answer. "No." Faith walked past him, across the room and headed straight into the bathroom.

The woman wasn't boring or predictable, that much was

certain. He shook his head with a chuckle and crawled into what he hoped was the *right* side of the bed and waited.

He didn't have to wait long this time before the bathroom door opened. The room was dark, but he watched her shadow approach the bed before he felt the gentle dip of the mattress as she laid down.

"I could sleep on the —"

"You're fine." She cut him off. "In fact, it's kind of nice having you here."

"It is?"

She laughed.

There was something about the dark that maybe allowed Faith to drop her guard. He couldn't be sure, but whatever it was, she seemed a lot more relaxed than she had in... well...days.

"I like that sound."

"What's that?"

"Your laughter. It's...pretty." He answered honestly. "And you didn't seem very happy tonight."

He still couldn't see her face, but he could tell she'd tensed and the smile he'd been sure was on her face had likely slipped away.

"Sorry, Faith. I didn't mean to make you—"

"You didn't make me anything, Logan. It's just been...well, all a little unexpected. And to tell you the truth, I don't really want to talk about it right now."

If he'd been surprised by her before, he was downright shocked when she reached across the empty bed between them and trailed her fingers down his chest.

He froze for a second, not sure that she'd meant the touch, or more specifically, what it meant.

"Logan?"

"Yes?"

"I need you."

Fuck. He didn't need to be asked twice. Not by Faith. But still, something wasn't right. *She* wasn't right.

He moved closer to her and trailed his hand down her bare arm. *Was she naked?*

She shivered under his touch and he rested his hand on her hip, letting his fingers fan out over her curves.

"Logan?"

"Faith, are you—"

She moved so suddenly and silenced him with a kiss that he didn't have time to form any reaction other than wrapping his arms around her and holding her close as he rolled to his back and deepened the kiss with her on top of him. His hands slid down her back.

Yes. She was definitely naked.

Damn.

There were probably a million things going on with her. All things that he should probably stop and talk to her about, but…she was kissing him and his body was responding. Urgently.

She groaned and wiggled herself down onto his growing hardness.

"You're sure?" He pulled away long enough to ask.

"So sure." She kissed him again.

Logan ran his hands down the length of her, taking in every inch of her soft skin until his hands landed on her perfectly round ass. He cupped her and squeezed before flipping her easily and smoothly onto her back so he could straddle her.

He wished for light so he could see her beauty beneath him and the way her breasts would be heaving with the need for him. But there was no way he was leaving her, not even to open the blinds across the room to let the moonlight in. There was no way he was going to break whatever spell they were currently under.

Instead, he shimmied out of his boxer shorts before once more bending to kiss her.

She moaned again as he slipped a hand down and between her legs, finding her wet and ready for him.

"Logan." Her fingers dug into his ass and pressed him forward with an urgency he was more than happy to answer.

A moment later, he'd shifted between her legs and pressed himself into her wet heat, taking his time in an effort to enjoy every second, but she was restless and demanding. Faith pulled him closer to her, wanting more, and despite his best efforts, he couldn't deny her.

"Harder, Logan."

Two words, but they sent a shock wave of desire through him as he obeyed her command and entered her again, harder, until they were both moaning together as they jointly reached their peaks. And then they were crashing over the crest together, coming hard with an intensity that left them each breathless.

When he could think straight again, he bent and kissed her softly, hoping more than anything that he could convey all the things he felt for her, because he hadn't yet been able to bring himself to say them aloud. She was more than a bet. She was more than a late-night fuck in the dark. So much more.

He reached up to brush the hair from her face but her cheek was wet. *Was she crying?*

"Faith?" Logan leaned back and rolled off to the side, but unwilling to let her go yet, kept one hand on her hip to hold her close. "Are you okay?"

Again, he wished for light so he could see what was going on on her beautiful face. But he wouldn't leave her side.

"I'm fine." She sniffed. "I was just…" She chuckled a little and her voice changed. "I guess I lost, Logan."

"Lost what?"

"The bet."

No.

"I lost."

"You didn't." He laughed. "Quite the opposite, I'd say." He let his hand travel up her body so his fingers could trace the side of her breast.

She relaxed under his touch briefly before tensing. "I did," she said. "I lost. I can't pretend anymore. It's not right. Stephanie doesn't deserve to be lied to. It was one thing before we got to know her, but she's sweet and she's our friend and...I lost. You win."

He won.

Logan let that roll around his head. "So that means..."

"One night," she said, reminding him of his terms should he win the bet that he'd only made to get close to her in the first place. "That was your prize, right?"

There was something in her voice he didn't like. Something that sent alarm bells ringing.

"And you got it. We're even. I'll tell her the truth in the morning."

Chapter Fourteen

IT HAD BEEN AN INCREDIBLY long night. Faith had never been so aware of another person's presence than with Logan lying right next to her in the bed. She knew she'd been terrible. Hurtful and mean and...she regretted everything almost immediately. *Everything.*

Saying what she'd said. Having sex with him.

Ugh.

That had been wrong, and she knew it even at the time. When she'd come to bed, she'd had no intention of that happening, but it was almost as if the moment he'd opened his mouth to talk to her, as though he'd been concerned about her, something melted. It was selfish and wrong and it only made her feel even worse about everything, but in that moment, she'd just needed one more time with him. One more opportunity to feel the way he made her feel. It wasn't fair, and she regretted it deeply.

But mostly, she'd regretted ever letting herself feel anything for Logan in the first place. It would have been so much easier if she could have just kept hating him.

No. Not hating him.

Being annoyed by him?

Keeping him at arm's length?

Dammit.

It didn't matter. She *did* have feelings for him.

But it couldn't work.

She'd come to that conclusion after leaving Hope earlier. Everything her sister said should have changed her mind. It should have made her realize that she *could* allow herself to have feelings for a man. And maybe it did. But with Logan? He didn't feel the same way. She was nothing more than a bet to him. A challenge. A conquest that he could add to his list. Maybe she was ready to start opening up her heart, but she knew enough to know that she still needed to protect it, too. From Logan.

Maybe she hadn't been fair the night before, but Logan hadn't corrected her either. When she'd told him the game was over and that he'd won, he hadn't said anything to make her think any different. Because she'd been right. And maybe that was the part that hurt the most. As much as she didn't want to admit it, some small part of her had hoped she was wrong. Which was why she needed distance. As much as it hurt, it was the best choice for everyone that she pushed him away. And oh, it did hurt.

Faith had been pushing men away her entire life and it always sucked. In fact, there were one or two occasions when it had even been hard. But it had never made her feel the way she was feeling now.

She'd woken early, hoping to get out of the house before Logan got up. Not that she'd slept much, but she'd obviously drifted off at some point because when she had opened her eyes, Logan was already gone.

That should have made her happy, or at least given her some sense of relief. Instead, it only made her heart ache. She needed to shake it off.

Faith couldn't remember the last time she'd put on running clothes and worked out. Definitely not since she'd been back in Glacier Falls, but it was the only thing she could think of to get out of her head.

She pushed her body hard as she ran through the wooded trails around their property, dodging trees, rocks, and roots on the paths. It was a good workout, and by the time she'd been out just over an hour, she'd worked up quite a sweat. But still she was restless as she held her side and walked across the yard toward the house. Despite a cramp in her side, the exertion hadn't helped her work out any of her feelings—quite the opposite, really—and Faith was tempted to turn around and run some more when Stephanie, who had been sitting on the porch, waved and called out to her.

"Faith! I'm so glad you're back. I've been up all night."

That makes two of us.

Faith took one last longing look at the trees behind her and headed for the porch.

"Ideas, huh?" She collapsed into a chair, suddenly feeling as though she couldn't walk another foot, let alone a mile. "Tell me everything."

Stephanie, who must have been up all night looking at Pinterest and dreaming about the perfect elopement ceremony, spent the next twenty minutes telling Faith all of her ideas, or thoughts about flowers, decorations, and dresses, finally finishing with, "I mean, I don't really know if I need any of that. I'd be happy to get married in a sweat suit if that's what's available, you know? I just want to do it."

Faith turned and examined her new friend. Something seemed a little off about Stephanie at the moment, but maybe it was just her lack of sleep, or her own jaded thoughts. "You okay?"

Stephanie nodded, her red hair bouncing in its ponytail.

"I'm just...well, I love Dax. I do. And I want to get married, but..."

"You don't have to do this." Faith sat up in her chair. "Not if it doesn't feel right. There's no rule that says you—"

"No!" Steph shook her head hard. "It's not like that. It's not like I don't know about Dax. I do...it's just...it's nothing." She looked past Faith, out to the trees and mountains. "I really like being around you guys. Seeing true love like what Hope and Levi have, and you and Logan...it's inspiring, you know? Like all relationships should be. So strong. So honest, and true."

Honest and true.

"You can see it just by looking at the two of you, there's so much pure adoration between the two of you and it really is inspiring. Does that make sense?"

It didn't. Because Faith was a big fat liar, and she needed to tell Stephanie the truth before it went any further. She took a deep breath. "There's something I need to tell you, Steph. I probably should have—"

The other woman held up a hand to stop her. "I just need to say one more thing."

Faith nodded and let her continue.

"I wanted to thank you, Faith, because seeing the love you and Logan have just makes everything so clear. And watching the two of you, I know there's a chance. After all, if a love as raw and obvious as the two of you can finally be realized after what you've both been through..." She shook her head and laughed. "Well, it gives the rest of us hope, you know? And I think that's what we all need right now. Thank you."

There was so much more to what Stephanie said than she was letting on, but it made one thing perfectly clear to Faith. There was no way she could tell her the truth about Logan. Not yet. Not now. Not when there was obviously something going on with her. She seemed conflicted about her own wedding and relationship. If Steph was looking to her for inspiration, she was definitely not going to be the one to burst her bubble, not now. It wouldn't be fair.

"Anyway," Stephanie ran her hands over her head, smoothing her hair back, "I just needed to get that off my chest, because I really do appreciate you. What is it you were going to say?"

Faith swallowed hard and closed her eyes, searching for something to say instead of the truth that was burning up her tongue. "I was going to tell you about the craziest thing. It's kind of a secret I've been holding onto for a long time and well, I just told Hope, so in case you're wondering what's going on, it's that apparently our mother had a baby about three years before we were born and gave it up for adoption."

She hadn't meant to say anything. They'd decided not to. After all, it was a family matter and really none of anyone else's business, but it had just kind of slipped out. She really needed to get a hold of herself. Or get some sleep. Or just generally pull herself together.

"What?" Stephanie's mouth slowly dropped open. "You have a sister out there?"

"Half-sister." Faith nodded. "We don't really know much. I found a few papers that my mom must have requested from the adoption agency when the baby turned eighteen, but they don't tell us much. Just that the baby was born in Calgary in September of 1991."

All of the blood drained from Stephanie's face, and for a moment, Faith was sure she was going to pass out. She jumped to her feet and crossed the porch to where Steph was sitting. "Are you okay? What's—"

"I was born in Calgary in September of 1991, Faith. I was adopted in a closed adoption. I never knew anything about my birth parents and—"

"There's no way." Faith took a step back. She hadn't even

considered the possibility that Stephanie Starz, the world's biggest movie star, was their adopted older sister. *No. Way.*

She shook her head. "That doesn't make any sense. You said you grew up in Northern Canada."

"I did. But I was born in Calgary. That's all I know." The color slowly returned to Stephanie's face, the pallor replaced by rosy cheeks as she grew more excited. "I don't really want to ask my mom." She shook her head. "She gets sensitive about it and when I started starring in movies, she got really worried that details of the adoption would get out and people would come around, insisting they were my birth parents."

"I could see that."

"Right? It makes sense. But Mom always said she didn't know much about my birth mother and she'd asked the agency, but the records had been destroyed in a flood a few years after I was born. I guess they weren't on computers yet." She shrugged. "And to be honest, I've never really cared all that much. But now..." Her eyes grew wide again.

Her *green* eyes. Hope and Faith's eyes were blue, like their dad's. But her mom's... Was there any family resemblance?

Blonde hair versus fiery red? *No.*

Short and petite versus tall and curvy? *No.*

The feeling as though they'd all known each other forever? *Yes.*

Was that enough?

Faith shook her head slowly. It could be possible. It might be crazy enough to be actually true.

She laughed and Steph joined in.

"I think we need to go talk to Hope."

"I don't believe it." Hope shook her head again. "I just don't believe it."

"Hope? Maybe you should lay down for a minute." Faith had been watching her sister carefully, and she might be telling them that she wasn't getting worked up but her face showed otherwise, and she was definitely not going to be held responsible for any high blood pressure issues in her pregnant and sick sister. No way. "You look a little—"

"Blown away?" Hope waved her away. "Because I am. Do you really think that you could be our *sister*? That's so crazy."

"It *is* crazy." Faith worked hard to be the calm and somewhat reasonable one in the room. "Especially because we have no proof and no actual details about anything. Just because Stephanie was born in the same place on the same day and given up for adoption does not mean—wait a minute." Faith turned to Steph. "What day *were* you born?" They hadn't actually discussed dates, just the month and the year.

Stephanie beamed and turned to Hope, who was listening intently. "September 28, 1991."

But her smile quickly fell away at Hope's reaction. Faith watched as her sister's face transformed, the excitement and hope replaced by disappointment and reality. "No," Hope said quietly. "Our sister was born on September 2, 1991. Close. But…"

"I guess close doesn't count when you're talking about birthdays?"

"Not in this case."

Stephanie's shoulders had caved in and she looked as if she might crumple, so Faith moved to put an arm around her and hug her into her side. "It's okay, Steph. It was totally farfetched, anyway. And it doesn't change the fact that we're all new friends, right?"

"No." Steph shook her head and tried to force a smile. "But honestly, I let myself believe just for a second that I had a family who loved me. Sisters. And…"

"Hey." Hope struggled to sit up. "You *do* have a family who loves you. And you have us. Just because the birthdays don't line up, doesn't change that we're friends and we care about you. And heck, it's close, right? Maybe if we can't find our actual sister, we could just kind of adopt you in unofficially."

Faith's heart broke for the woman as Stephanie tried not to let her disappointment show. "I'm sorry," she said. "I never should have said anything. I didn't mean to get everyone excited, and…well, I just didn't think. And—"

"Hey." Steph shook her head and in a flash, the frown was gone, replaced by the brilliant smile that had made her famous. "It's not your fault," she said. "It's not anyone's fault. It's just…" She shrugged again and turned quickly from the sisters. "I think I'm going to go for a walk. I'll be back in a bit."

"Of course."

They let her go. Faith didn't know her that well yet, but she knew enough to know that Steph would reach out if she wanted to talk. They didn't speak until they heard the front door click shut downstairs.

Maybe it was the sound, or just something else inside her, that finally felt like too much, but Faith sat down hard on her sister's bed and dropped her head against her chest. It had been a long day, but it wasn't even noon yet.

"What's going on with you?" Hope asked after a minute. "Because I know it doesn't have anything to do with our long-lost sister. I just didn't think you were that invested."

"I'm not," she answered honestly. "At least I wasn't. But it would have been pretty cool if it was Stephanie, right?" She managed a smile, but Hope wasn't buying it.

"Seriously. What's going on with you? You look like someone just ran over your puppy, and you haven't had a dog since we were kids." It was a lame attempt at a joke, but it made Faith smile nonetheless.

She hadn't intended on saying anything to Hope, but it seemed to be the day for saying things she shouldn't be saying, and there didn't seem to be much point in keeping it from her either, so, with a sigh, Faith told her sister, "I broke up with Logan."

"You what?"

"Well, I guess that's the best way to describe it, even though we weren't really dating or anything. It's all just…" To her horror, tears sprung from her eyes and once they started, she couldn't stop them. And she didn't even try.

Hope sat in silence for a few minutes and let her sister cry. Finally, she reached out and squeezed Faith's leg. "You need to stop, Faith."

She looked up and swiped at her nose. "Stop crying?"

"No." Hope laughed. "Stop pushing people away. Specifically, Logan."

"That's not fair," she said, quick to defend herself. "You don't even know what happened."

"I don't need to." Hope sat back against the headboard. "I know that he has feelings for you. And you have feelings for him. That scares the hell out of you, so you push him away."

"I don't." She shook her head, needing to get her sister's words out of her brain. She was wrong. It wasn't like that. It was that they weren't compatible. *They could never work. They weren't meant to be together. They never had been. They…* "Shit." The realization hit her hard. "I do," she said, more to herself than Hope. "But I don't know why." She sniffed hard and looked to her sister for an answer. "Why do I do that? Why do I push so hard?"

Hope's smile was kind despite the fact that she probably wanted to smack her sister senseless for being so obtuse. "I think it all makes sense now."

"What makes sense?"

Hope nodded to herself. "This was it, wasn't it?"

She looked at her sister sideways.

"This was what changed everything for you. When we were

126

kids. You were young and impressionable and completely influenced by overhearing that argument. To the point where it changed everything."

It was. It was the one moment in a sensitive time for a young Faith. In that instant, watching her parents who claimed to love each other more than anyone else in the world speak so cruelly to each other, everything shifted. Faith locked away a piece of her heart that day and from then on, she refused to let herself love or even believe in the concept of it. After all, why would she want to expose herself to that kind of pain?

She shrugged in response to her sister's comment. It seemed so trivial when her sister said it out loud. After all, everyone fought, right? It wasn't a deal breaker or a relationship ender. At least, it didn't have to be.

"You got scared that someone who loved you more than anyone and anything else in the world could have the ability to hurt you so badly. The way Mom and Dad hurt each other with the truth of the adoption. If you let someone love you like that, you give them the power to hurt you, too. It's very vulnerable."

She couldn't disagree with anything. "Then why would you let someone love you if you knew they could hurt you?" Faith asked honestly. "Why would you open yourself up to that?"

"That's easy." Hope smiled so wide, it lit up her entire face. "Because the love is so great, it's worth the risk. A million times over, it's worth it. And I think you're missing the biggest point of all, Faith."

She tilted her head and listened.

"Mom may have kept a crazy big secret and they may have had a huge knock-down fight about it where they said terrible things, but what you've chosen to ignore all of these years is that even though that happened, it didn't break them. It didn't destroy everything they'd built together, because they loved each other so deeply, they couldn't be broken. Not ever. And that's the real magic. If you let yourself love…" she paused, letting it sink in, "you're giving yourself the greatest gift you possibly could."

Faith knew her sister was trying to help, but she couldn't possibly understand. The secret between their parents *had* stayed with them. That night and that fight, it had broken their relationship and instead of owning that, they just continued to act as if nothing was wrong and that they were perfectly in love and the very definition of romance. It was a lie. All of it.

As if she knew what Faith was going to say, Hope scooted closer to her on the bed. "But I don't think this is why you've closed your heart, Faith."

"What?"

"You're smart enough to know that people fight and they make up. You've always been smart enough to know that."

She opened her mouth to object, but Hope was on a roll. "There is no way you've been jaded and bitter about love this whole time because of that. But I think I know what it is."

Faith tilted her head. "Do you now?"

"I do." Hope's grin couldn't be contained. "You're scared." She nodded, pleased with herself. "Loving someone and opening your heart to someone else is the most vulnerable thing you can do. And you've simply been scared." She smacked her palm to her forehead. "It's so painfully simple that I never saw it, but you, my sweet sister, are a big, giant scaredy-cat. What if you love Logan and he doesn't love you back?"

Her words hit her in the gut, but she couldn't deny them. What was the point?

"What if you're right?"

"I *am* right!" Hope almost vibrated with excitement. "I knew it."

Faith shook her head and looked down at the bedspread. "I don't want to get hurt, Hope. I don't know if I could handle it."

"You could." She reached for her sister's hand and squeezed. "You could handle anything. You know that. Stop hiding. Besides, protecting your heart from hurting might save you from a potentially excruciating pain, but it also stops you from experiencing the greatest form of pleasure and happiness. There is no gain without risk. And that's no way to live."

Faith let her words sink in.

"Oh, Faith. Why didn't you tell me any of this? Why did you keep this inside?" She shook her sister's hand.

"I wanted to protect you, Hope. I didn't want you to hurt, too."

Her sister pulled her into a tight hug. "Now it's my turn to make sure you don't keep hurting, Faith. You deserve love, sis. More than anyone else I know, you deserve it. And now that I know everything, I can't keep sitting back watching you hurt yourself so badly by keeping love away." She pulled back and looked her in the eyes. "You don't know it yet, but by keeping Logan at a distance, you're robbing yourself of so much."

When she didn't say anything right away, Hope added, "Think about it, Faith. I mean, really think about it. Okay?"

She nodded and after a moment she spoke, her voice little more than a whisper. "But what if I'm the only one, Hope? I mean, I've always been a game to Logan and with this bet…"

"You know you're more than that to Logan." Hope's voice was stern. "You know that."

She shrugged. She thought she'd known that. But…it was so hard to know what was true or not. And even if he did have feelings for her, too…

A tear slipped down her cheek. "I think it's too late," she said softly. "I think I finally got what I thought I wanted and pushed him away for good."

Hope released her from the hug.

Chapter Fifteen

LOGAN HAD BEEN AVOIDING Faith for the last few days. Not because he didn't want to see her; he did. Badly. He also wanted answers. Answers that he deserved, goddammit. But he knew he wasn't going to get them. Not yet. He knew Faith well enough to know that if he pressed her, she would shut down. Just as she had the other night after they'd made love and she'd told him it was over and turned her back on him.

He'd tried, but there'd been nothing more he could say to get her to talk to him and tell him exactly what was really going on. Faith was a champion at shutting down and shutting him out.

He'd spent as much time as possible out of the house: mowing the yard, tending to gardens, fixing fences, staining deck boards. Pretty much anything that was on the list of things that *should* be done at some point. They all of a sudden became priorities on his to-do list. Anything that kept him out of the house.

At night, he usually made some sort of excuse about going to check on his mom or spending time with her because she was lonely. Logan was a strong man, but he didn't think that even he was strong enough to lie next to Faith in bed and not be able to touch her or talk to her or…

So he'd slept at his childhood home, in the bed he'd spent so many nights before. Only now it felt wrong. And it no longer felt like his bed or that he belonged there.

He belonged back at Ever After Ranch in Faith Turner's bed, holding her in his arms as her heart slowed after their lovemaking that had left them both breathless. *That* was where he belonged. Without a doubt.

The only problem was, he had no idea how he was going to get back there.

"Hello? Earth to Logan." Next to him at the airport, Levi snapped his fingers and pulled Logan from his trance. The trance he seemed to be perpetually in. "Maybe you should wait in the car." Levi shook his head. "I've been trying to talk to you for five minutes and you haven't even acknowledged me. You're kind of useless to me out here right now, you know?"

"Sorry." He meant it. "I'm here. I was just daydreaming. But I'm good now. What were you saying?"

Levi laughed. They'd made the trip into the city to pick up Dax Combs for the wedding that was supposed to take place the next evening. They'd been given strict instructions to keep everything on the *down low* and use as much subtlety as possible so as not to attract attention. Not that Logan had any idea how they were going to do that given how high profile the man was, but he'd try. For Stephanie's sake. Just like everyone else in the family, he'd come to really care about her. And just like everyone else, he couldn't help but feel disappointed that she wasn't Faith and Hope's long-lost sister. It had been a long shot, for sure, but still. It would have been kind of perfect.

"I was just wondering what you think this guy will be like?" Levi laughed. "Will he be all rich and famous arrogant asshole, or will he be more like Stephanie? Frankly, I always forget she's a mega star. She just seems like one of us. A Glacier Falls native."

"I agree. It seems so funny now in hindsight that Faith and I were so worried about pretending to be a couple just to impress her. The wedding of the century." He shook his head. "Pretty dumb, right?"

"Not dumb," Levi said seriously. "Honestly, you know I don't agree with the whole lying thing, but I know why you did it. And I think that's pretty special."

Logan knew his cousin was talking about how they'd lied to get the business and put Ever After on the map. But that wasn't really the truth.

"I did it to get close to Faith," he admitted. "Everything else was just going to be a bonus."

"I know." Levi looked to the glass sliding doors as a flight announcement was made. Dax would be coming through soon.

"You know?"

Levi smiled and nodded before turning to look at him. "Of course I know. We all know. And I stand by what I said—it's pretty special."

"Special that I wanted to get close to Faith?"

Levi nodded.

"Is it special that I fucked it all up?"

"You didn't."

"You know I did."

"No." Levi crossed his arms. "You didn't. Sure, it's not all going to plan right now, but that doesn't mean you fucked it up."

"I love her." The moment the words slipped past his lips, Logan knew it was true. He'd lusted after Faith for years, enjoyed messing with her, and making her crazy, but *love*? That was new. And it was true. "I do," he said with conviction. "I am completely in love with her. I think I always have been. It's not just a bet for me, Levi. It never was."

The arrival doors opened and closed, a few passengers slipping through, but Levi wasn't paying attention. He was looking directly at Logan as if he'd completely lost his mind. "I know, Logan," he said slowly. "I've always known. You've been desperately in love with Faith Turner almost as long as I've been in love with her sister. It just took you a lifetime to figure it out for yourself."

There was so much he wanted to say. *Years? A lifetime?* Logan struggled to get the words out, before finally opening his mouth to tell his cousin how wrong he was. But before he could say anything, Levi punched him in the arm.

"Holy shit. There he is."

He stepped forward toward a man wearing jeans, a T-shirt, and black leather jacket. He had dark sunglasses on despite the fact that he was inside. If he was supposed to be trying to keep a low profile, it definitely wasn't working. Not that anything about the man suggested that he was.

Logan swallowed back the words he'd been about to say to his cousin as he watched Levi approach Dax. There was no point in finishing the conversation anyway, because even though he'd been about to protest and declare that Levi was an idiot and didn't know what he was talking about, there was no point. It would have been a lie.

Levi was right.

Logan had been deeply in love with Faith for as long as he could remember.

The only difference between all the other times she'd pushed him away and now was that he'd finally had a taste of what being with Faith could be like. And he wasn't going to let it go so easily this time.

"So, you're getting married tomorrow. How's that feel?"

Getting Dax in the car without attracting too much attention had been harder than Logan had thought. Despite the fact that Dax himself didn't seem too fussed about attracting attention. He spoke loudly in the airport and more than once Logan had to cut him off before he said the name of the town they were taking him to. Stephanie had been clear. She didn't want anyone to know about the wedding. It was important to her to have a low-key elopement. So that's what she would have. Not that her fiancé seemed too worried about it, the way he was carrying on in public.

Regardless, they had him in the car now and were finally making their way out of the city and back to the mountains. Dax looked up from his phone long enough to answer Logan's question. "It doesn't feel any way, I guess. As long as it makes Steph happy, that's all that matters."

In the front seat, Levi and Logan exchanged glances. "But you want to get married?" Levi asked.

Dax answered with a shrug. "Doesn't really matter either way, I guess. Like I said, if it makes her happy, that's what it's all about, right? You guys know. You have women."

Again, they exchanged a glance, but it was Levi who spoke. "I agree about making your woman happy, but marriage… well, it's definitely one of those things that you should both be one hundred percent into. At least, in my opinion."

"Agreed." Logan grinned. "And from my limited experience in the wedding business, I'd say that applies all across the board."

Still, Dax shrugged and looked back to his phone. A few minutes later, he looked up. "What do you guys know about this super tiny, super-fast wedding she wants? Like, two months ago, she wanted the full blow-out with all our friends and family and everything. Like a four-page spread in *People* magazine, ya know? Eloping won't get us that kind of publicity."

That's the point.

As much as Logan had taken an instant disliking to the man, he was still Stephanie's fiancé, and also, a client. There was nothing to be gained by making him an enemy or making things any harder on Steph than was necessary. So instead of saying what he really wanted to, Logan turned around in the passenger seat. "This is more romantic," he said. "Intimate and special, with just the two of you. And if it's publicity you want, then later, when you share the photos, they'll blow up because everyone will be so surprised that the two of you eloped. It'll be big news. The wedding of the century that flew under the radar. It'll be huge."

He must have said the right thing, because Dax put down his phone and for the first time since he'd arrived, looked interested. "Do you think so?"

Both men in the front seat nodded. "For sure. And," Logan continued, "then Steph's happy too. And that's a win-win."

Dax seemed pleased with that idea and for the next thirty minutes of the drive chatted about New Zealand, and the film he was shooting. He mentioned his costar, Natalie Fear, quite a few times, which was probably normal considering they'd spent so much time together over the last few months, but Logan couldn't help but think it was a little odd that he didn't talk about his bride-to-be very much. Even when Logan tried to prompt him with questions, Dax skated over the details and went back to talking about movie production and what a blockbuster his latest film would be.

Logan certainly didn't have a ton of experience with celebrities—none, really—so he tried to give Dax the benefit of the doubt, but he couldn't help but feel like the man was nothing like Steph had described. She'd spoken about a sweet, doting man who was also not a fan of the fame that had been foisted on them. The man currently in the back of their SUV headed toward Glacier Falls and his bride was nothing like that. If anything, he was the exact opposite. Logan really didn't want to judge the man too harshly, but his first impressions of Dax Combs were that he was a grade-A asshole and not at all worthy of marrying his new friend.

Not that he could say anything.

What would he say?

As soon as they pulled up into the yard at Ever After, the door to the house opened and Stephanie, red hair flying behind her, came running outside.

Logan and Levi watched as the man they'd just spent the last few hours with transformed before their eyes.

"There's my little firecracker!" Dax yelled and, in two broad steps, crossed the distance toward his bride, wrapped her up tight in his arms, and swung her around in the most dramatic and movie-like scene Logan had ever witnessed in person.

The couple was still greeting each other with their tongues down each other's throats, when Logan grabbed the man's bags from the trunk and, together with Levi, walked around them to the porch, where Faith watched with wide eyes.

Logan tried to ignore the way his entire body stiffened the moment he caught sight of Faith. Or the way his stomach clenched or his breath caught in his throat. The full-body pull toward her was almost impossible to ignore, especially now that she'd…what? Broken up with him? Cast him out?

"That's quite a welcome." Faith laughed and shook her head a little. "You didn't have any issues picking him up?" The question was directed to both of them, but Logan couldn't help but notice she was looking directly at Levi when she asked.

"No issues," he answered. "But, Dax is…" He pressed his lips together and tilted his head.

"He's what?" She looked at Logan then, obviously searching for the answer. "Dax is—"

"Oh my God!" Stephanie interrupted them before Faith could get her answer. "Dax, you have to meet Faith." Stephanie dragged her fiancé across the yard and to the porch. "Faith is Logan's...girlfriend? Partner?"

Faith momentarily looked caught off guard, but she smiled and extended her hand to the celebrity. "Girlfriend," she said smoothly. "I'm Logan's girlfriend."

Girlfriend?

So, she obviously hadn't told Stephanie the truth yet then. *Interesting.*

Logan shot her a look, but she was steadfastly ignoring him, focusing instead on Dax, who was giving her a brilliant smile.

"Steph has told me so much about you," he said to her. "And already the welcome's been so great. I'm just beyond excited to get married to the love of my life here and what better place than this gorgeous ranch?"

Logan tried not to let his surprise show on his face, but one glance at his cousin told him he'd failed completely to hide his reaction.

Who the hell was this Dax?

He'd done a complete 180 since getting out of the car.

"It's going to be amazing," Faith said. "Why don't you come inside and we can go over some of the details before you rest up."

Levi led the way into the house, with Faith holding back.

She waited until they'd gone inside before turning around and facing him. "I didn't tell her yet."

"Obviously. So are we supposed to—"

"Maybe just keep your distance as much as possible until tomorrow. I'm not ruining her day when she's so excited, and now that Dax is here and just as excited, I don't think it's a good time to tell them the truth."

"About that." He wasn't going to say anything, but how could he not?

"About what?"

"Dax." Logan took a breath. "I don't think he's exactly… well, I don't know how to say this. But he was a totally different guy in the car. Like he didn't even care about Steph or the wedding. He was more interested in getting attention for the wedding and—"

"That's crazy, Logan. He's obviously totally obsessed with her. I'm sure it's just nerves and you guys just met. That would be weird."

"Maybe." Faith looked so sure, and what she said made some sense. Logan shrugged. "You're probably right. And really, it's not like I'm an expert on love or anything, right?"

He was joking, but the look on her face told him he'd hit a little closer to home than he'd intended. *Dammit.* "That's not really what I—"

"Forget it." She held up a hand to prevent him from saying anything more. "I can't do this right now, Logan. I just…" She pressed her mouth together, before biting her bottom lip.

She took a deep breath and Logan was positive she was going to say something important. Maybe how she'd been wrong and she didn't want him to keep his distance, or that maybe they could—

"I just…" She shook her head as her shoulders slumped in defeat of whatever she'd been about to say.

But he wasn't going to let her go that easy. Logan reached out and held her upper arm. "No. What were you going to say?"

She opened her mouth, but closed it again. The moment had passed and she pulled her arm out of his grip. "I should get inside."

Chapter Sixteen

STEPHANIE HADN'T BEEN able to sleep in. How could she? It was her wedding day and there was so much to do. She snuck out of bed before Dax could wake up and see her. It would be bad luck for him to see her on their wedding day, wouldn't it?

Damn.

She hadn't thought of that the night before. She hadn't thought of a lot of things. Like the time difference between the mountains and New Zealand. Dax had tried to stay up as long as possible in order to avoid jet lag if he could, but finally he'd insisted on going up to bed. Of course, she went with him and they'd made love before he'd fallen asleep next to her.

They hadn't been together in just over a month, and they were no strangers to time apart, but usually when they came back together, they couldn't keep their hands off each other and Dax would all but tear her clothes off the second they were alone.

Not last night. It had been different. A distance between them.

Steph stood in front of the bathroom mirror and stared at her reflection. She was a woman in love about to marry the man of her dreams. Yet, something wasn't right.

She didn't look right. Shouldn't she have a sparkle in her eye the way Hope did whenever Levi came in the room? Or the tiniest grin on her face that Faith seemed to get whenever Logan was nearby?

She leaned in and examined herself carefully, but all she could see were dark smudges under her eyes that definitely weren't sparkling.

It's only because she'd had such a restless sleep the night before, she told herself. *There was just so much going on.* Of course she was stressed out. And she was just overthinking everything because she'd been spending so much time with Faith and Hope and their men, who were…different than Dax. That's all it was. Different. Not better or worse. Just different.

Satisfied with her explanation to herself, Stephanie brushed her teeth and pulled her hair up into a ponytail before quickly getting dressed and sneaking out of the room.

It was early and no one else seemed to be up, so she measured out the coffee grounds, the way Logan had shown her a few days earlier. He'd laughed at her when she told him she didn't know how to make a pot of coffee and made a comment about Faith's complete ineptitude at making coffee. It was just one of many random similarities between her and the twins that might have been explained by the fact that they were long-lost sisters.

Except they weren't sisters.

Stephanie's shoulders slumped as the disappointment hit her fresh. It had been such a long shot, and what were the odds that it could have ever actually been true? Still, for a few minutes, she'd actually believed that she could be Faith and Hope's older sister. It had felt so right and so many of the details lined up. It made sense.

But of course it had been too good to be true.

Maybe that was part of what was making her feel down? She'd been so close to belonging to something. To a family. And then...

Stephanie shook her head hard. She was being ridiculous. She *had* a family. Her parents loved her. They'd adopted her and *wanted* her. They'd given her an amazing childhood. It wasn't until she'd become famous that things had become strained with them. When she'd started to bring in real money. More money then she'd ever known what to do with. In fact, Steph's first response had been to help them out. Buy them a big house, and new cars. Maybe a place down south so they wouldn't have to spend winters fighting the deep freeze of Northern Canada.

More than anything, she'd wanted to share her wealth, but they'd refused. They wouldn't take any of her money. The luxury SUVs she'd bought them had been donated to a local day care. *Donated.*

And when she'd called them, confused and hurt, her mom had tried to explain to her that they didn't want anything from her. That it should always be the other way around: the parents giving to their child, and her grand gifts made her father feel guilty and unworthy as a parent.

It was ridiculous. But not to them.

Even so, it had created a rift between them. As the years went on, and they'd refuse her offers to fly them down to Los Angeles for movie premieres or awards shows, Stephanie had started to feel more and more abandoned by them as they clearly didn't accept her lifestyle. Or more specifically, her father couldn't get over his pride long enough to be proud of her and what she'd created for herself.

The coffee finished brewing, so she poured herself a cup and took it outside to the porch, where she settled into the swing that had become one of her favorite places on the ranch.

Ever After had very quickly felt like home to her, and everyone like close friends that she didn't want to leave. But she'd have to, soon. She couldn't stay in Glacier Falls forever. Even if she wanted to.

Besides, she'd be a married woman, and she and Dax would return to LA and begin their married life together.

What would that look like?

She hadn't stopped to think about what things would be like after they got married. Would they both immediately get back to work? Dax still had filming to finish up on his current project and she'd been waffling between scripts. Her agent, Brenda, was starting to press her to choose one, and she would. Soon.

Maybe looking at the scripts again would take her mind off the wedding for a few minutes. Stephanie pulled her phone out of her pocket and flipped it on to download the files but before she could, her screen lit up with text messages from her assistant, Terri. Over the last few days, she'd started to reach out a little more so Terri wouldn't think she'd fallen off the face of the earth, but still, she'd kept her location a secret. And she planned to keep it that way for a little longer. At least until after the wedding.

With a sigh, she clicked open the first text.

What is this!?! Where ARE you!?! Who IS this!?!

The coffee went sour in her stomach, and Steph swallowed down a knot of fear. A text that asked those three questions with that many exclamation marks was never good. The picture attached was taking a bit to download—the cellular signal wasn't always strong in the mountains—but as far as

Stephanie was concerned, the photo didn't take long enough to develop on her screen because the moment it did, she knew she was in trouble.

Chapter Seventeen

"OKAY, OKAY." Faith was in full damage-control mode. "It's not that bad." She looked again at her tablet with the photo on full screen and shook her head.

Stephanie had forwarded her the photo that her assistant had shared with her earlier that morning.

"Not that bad?" Stephanie lifted her head from the table. "Seriously? How could you think it's not that bad?"

Faith looked at it again, with new eyes. It was a candid snapshot of Stephanie and Nick, Damon's friend from the city. They were sitting outside of Sweetie Pies, laughing, and from all outward appearances, having a great time. And that's how she'd seen it. But when she looked closer, and with a critical eye that obviously the tabloid had used, she noticed other things.

The way they were turned to each other, their knees almost touching.

The way Stephanie had her head thrown back in abandon.

Her hand on his arm, in what could definitely be seen as an affectionate gesture.

And most importantly, the look in Nick's eyes.

No matter what Faith knew to be true, there was no

denying what the picture *showed*. Which was a woman sharing a very cozy moment over coffee with a man.

A man who wasn't her fiancé.

"Okay," Faith finally relented. "I could see how a gossip magazine would be able to find something sinister with this picture. But you know it's not true." She turned to look at Stephanie and added, "It's not true, right? What they said?"

The accompanying headline had read: "*Stephanie Starz canoodling with sexy stranger. Where is Stephanie? And where is Dax?*"

"No!" She jumped up from her chair. "How could you even ask me that? Of course I wasn't *canoodling*. I just *met* him."

Her eyes flicked to the side and Steph glanced down quickly, but Faith didn't bother pushing that particular detail. Maybe she had just met Nick, but she'd obviously enjoyed that meeting. Still, Faith believed her friend. There was nothing untoward about it. She trusted that was true.

"Okay." She put her hand on Stephanie's back and led her back to the table. "I believe you and so will Dax. Just like you believe him when he tells you there's no truth to the garbage they print about him, right?"

Again, Stephanie's eyes flicked and she looked down.

"Right, Steph? You believe him, don't you?"

"Mostly," she offered finally. "It's complicated, but the media and the tabloids can really get to you after a while. They make you question things you never thought you would. They can get in your head."

"I bet they do."

Both women turned to see Logan walk in the front door.

"How are your mom's horses?" Faith asked quickly. They'd been making up a series of lies about how Logan was needed over at the Langdon ranch late at night and early in the morning so as not to admit the truth about their relationship yet. Faith still fully planned to tell Stephanie the truth, but with the wedding being planned so quickly, and now with this additional stress, it didn't seem right to own up yet.

"They're good," Logan answered smoothly. He crossed the kitchen to the coffee pot and turned to look in question at the women.

"She made it," Faith answered his unasked question and Logan chuckled.

"Forgive me," he said when he had a cup and was seated at the table across from the distressed actress. "I overheard a bit of what you were talking about and I can totally understand how it would all get in your head, but if I may, can I offer a quick piece of advice?"

Both women looked up and waited for his wisdom.

Logan took his time as he sipped his coffee before putting the mug down again. "If there is anything you're unsure about, Stephanie—anything that is giving you doubts, anything at all...it's not an awful idea to postpone the wedding."

"What?" Stephanie put both hands on the table and stared at Logan as if he'd lost his mind, which he clearly had if he was suggesting such an insane solution.

They'd never, ever advised a bride to call off a wedding. It wasn't their job to decide who should and should not get married. *What was he thinking?*

"You think I shouldn't marry Dax?"

"Yes. Well, no. I'm just saying..." Logan looked to Faith for help, but she just shook her head and glared at him.

He truly was losing his mind.

"I was just saying," Logan tried again. "That if there is any doubt or anything that is going to prevent you from having the best day of your life, you should deal with it beforehand. That's all."

His explanation seemed to settle her. At least for a moment.

Stephanie sat in silence for a few minutes, sipping her coffee and seemingly contemplating Logan's advice before she finally declared, "You're right. I'm going to talk to Dax right now. I need this all to be clear. Bad luck seeing the bride before the wedding, be damned. I need to be right in my mind. You're right."

Faith could see by the look on Logan's face that there was still something he wasn't saying, but she waited until Stephanie had left the room to go talk to her fiancé before she asked. "What's going on, Logan? Why would you ever suggest something like that to her? Are you crazy?"

He shook his head and pushed his coffee away. "Not at all. I don't think she should marry him. I told you yesterday, he's an asshole."

"Logan!" Faith hiss-whispered his name before she grabbed his arm and hauled him out on the porch where they couldn't be overheard. "What the —"

"I stand by what I said, Faith. Ask Levi. He'll agree with me. The man doesn't deserve her. He was a total douche at the airport, trying to get as much attention as he could when we were supposed to be subtle. And then when we got in the car, he was talking about Stephanie as if she were nothing more than a media opportunity. He doesn't want a quiet wedding. He wanted the big event because it would earn them a photo spread in *People* magazine and even more fame. I'm telling you, Faith. He's a total ass."

"No way." She shook her head. "I saw the way he greeted her. He loves her and missed her. I know he's excited about the wedding."

Logan crossed his arms. "He's an actor, Faith. He's acting. It's all a show. He's just really damn good at acting."

No way.

A man couldn't put it on like that. No way could he act as if he were madly in love with a woman when he didn't have real feelings. And make her believe it, too? *No.* No one was that good of an actor.

Her head snapped up and her eyes locked with Logan's as the reality of what was going on hit her.

A man *could* be that good of an actor. Logan had been.

Oh my God.

Maybe she'd been right all along and she was nothing more than a game to him? She couldn't bear it. Not now. Hope was wrong. She wasn't strong. Not when it came to this. She blinked hard, willing herself not to cry. She couldn't let herself lose control. Opening up her heart was only going to cause hurt. Hell, she hadn't even let him in yet, and the pain was already almost too much.

Her stomach roiled, the coffee she'd drank going sour in her gut as it all became crystal-clear. As much as she wanted her feelings to be reciprocated, her first instinct had been right.

"Just like you, you mean?"

"What?" Logan dropped his arms and stared at her. "What do you mean?"

She took a breath and all of a sudden wanted him to feel what she was feeling. She wanted him to hurt, too. "Dax is a really good actor," she said, each word a dagger shot in his direction. "Just like you are, right, Logan?"

"What the—"

"You actually made me believe it was real and that we might really have something together. And the worst part is, for a minute, I even wanted it to be."

"Faith, I—"

"You are a pretty fuckin' good actor, too, Logan. Maybe Dax can get you a role in his new film because clearly you have that in common. And of course you'd recognize a five-star performance when you saw it. You've been giving one of your own this whole time. And I fell for it." She shook her head and willed herself not to cry. She knew she was being a first-class bitch and that was the point. If she pushed hard enough this time, she could keep him away for good.

"Faith, don't." He looked sad and confused and angry, all at the same time. "Don't do this. Don't keep doing this. You're—"

"Done." She finished for him. "I'm totally done. For a minute, I let myself think that maybe I could let myself...it doesn't matter. I'm done now, Logan. I have to be."

Her body yearned to reach out to him. To let him pull her into his arms and tell her he wasn't acting. He did have feelings for her and he was sorry he'd ever let her believe otherwise. And for a second, she almost gave in to her heart. But then his face shifted again, this time anger winning out.

"You're done, are you?" He crossed his arms and glared at her. "*You* are done?" He laughed, but there was no humor in it. "All summer, I've done everything I can for you. I've busted my ass for Ever After and you while my mom was on her own with our ranch. Did you even know that she was going to sell it?" He didn't give her a chance to answer. "No. You didn't. Because it's always been about you, Faith." He shook his head. "And I didn't mind." For a moment, his voice lost the edge of anger as he spoke. "Because I would have..." He shook his head. "But I guess it doesn't matter."

It did! It did matter! But how could she say that now?

"I'm not perfect. I've made mistakes. Big ones. But...you think I'm just like Dax Combs?"

Again, she didn't have a chance to answer.

"Well, if you really think that, then you don't know me very well. And if that's the case, then it's me who's done, Faith."

Before she could say anything or ask him what he meant, or what he would have done, he spun on his heel and left her standing on the porch.

She stared after him for a minute before taking a deep breath. *Hope was wrong. It wasn't worth it.*

There was a reason she didn't open herself up. It just hurt too damn much.

He didn't want to walk away. But it was the right decision.

He needed space to think. He hadn't been expecting her to lose control like that. And he really hadn't expected her to admit that she had feelings for him. He'd suspected...hell, he *knew* she did. But for her to actually say it, that was something else.

You actually made me believe it was real and that we might really have something together. And the worst part is, for a minute, I even wanted it to be.

Of course he'd made her believe that. Because *he* believed it.

Dammit.

He slowed his breathing as he walked to his truck and calmed his thoughts.

She was the most bloody difficult woman he'd ever met. That much was very true. But he loved her. He always had. And he wasn't going to let her go. Not this time. No matter how much of a pain in the ass she was, she was *his* pain in the ass. He just needed to prove it to her.

He pressed his hands against the hood of his truck and dropped his head down.

The whole situation had opened his eyes. Stephanie. Dax. The bet. Faith's outburst. All of it.

She thought he was acting? He'd prove to her he wasn't and he never had been.

"I don't know what the hell is going on out here this morning, but it's frickin' chaos."

Logan jerked his head up as Levi's voice came up behind him. He turned to see his cousin striding toward him.

"Steph's crying. Dax is...I'm not sure what he's doing, but it's dramatic. Faith looks like she's...well, I'm not really sure what's going on here now." He shot Logan a look, but he definitely wasn't getting into it now. "And Hope is going on about something not being right with the marriage license. Honestly, today is not a good day for whatever it is that's going on with you. I'm sorry, cousin, but it's going to have to wait. Come on. Let's go."

"Go?" Logan shook his head, trying to follow along with what Levi was saying. "Go where?"

Levi laughed. "The ceremony site." He looked at him pointedly and when Logan still didn't respond, he continued, "Get the music ready, the arch, the glasses for the toast... you know? Wedding stuff? Please don't tell me that you've forgotten how to do it all now that I'm home."

"No." He shook his thoughts clear. "Of course not. I just thought that..."

He wasn't sure what he'd thought. Maybe that the wedding was postponed or that Steph had changed her mind and wasn't going to marry that asshole after all. Or maybe he'd seen the article, and it was Dax who had pulled the plug? Whatever he *had* thought, it certainly hadn't been that the wedding was actually going to happen.

"I don't know what you thought." Levi slapped him on the back and held out his hand for the keys. "But whatever it is, you're clearly not thinking at all right now. I'll drive."

He handed them over and ran his hands over his face.

"We're also supposed to go down to the registry and see what the problem is with the license," Levi said as he opened the door. "But first, I think you need some coffee. And maybe a breakfast sandwich. You don't look..." He waved his hand in search of a description, but Logan wasn't interested in his cousin's assessment.

"Whatever." He got in the passenger side of his own truck and slammed the door. "Drive."

Chapter Eighteen

THE CEREMONY WAS LESS than an hour away and still, Faith hadn't heard from Logan or Levi about what the holdup was with the marriage license. She'd tried not to worry Stephanie with the details of it all because the poor woman was stressed enough about everything. After her freak-out earlier, she'd broken her own rule of seeing her groom before the wedding and gone to explain the photo in the tabloid to Dax.

Not that he'd seemed very concerned about it. In fact, he'd thought it was funny. His exact words being, "Like I'm actually worried about a tech geek stealing my woman."

Faith wasn't the only one put off by his choice of words; Stephanie, too, had looked annoyed. But the moment Dax told her how much he loved her and pulled her in for a kiss, everything seemed to be forgotten.

Maybe Logan was right. Maybe he was just a really good actor.

But it also might be the stress of the wedding causing him to act a little strange. She may not have been doing it for long, but Faith had seen enough brides and grooms who were normally very chill and easygoing turn into crazy people on the morning of their big day to know it was a real thing. Weddings, no matter what size they were, even the tiny, intimate ones, were stressful.

Which was why she really didn't want to have to tell Steph about the license issue. But no marriage license meant no actual marriage. It was definitely an issue that would have to be sorted out.

There was no putting it off any longer. Faith grabbed a bottle of prosecco and a few glasses and headed upstairs to find the bride-to-be.

She needn't have worried so much, because before she even got all the way down the hall to Stephanie's room, she could hear the laughter and when she set foot inside, instead of being greeted with a sobbing, stressed-out mess, Stephanie was laughing along with something Hope had said.

Hope was settled into the armchair by the window, looking quite pleased with herself.

"I guess we don't need this after all." Faith set the bottle down, but Hope waved her hand.

"Are you kidding? The bride always deserves a few bubbles before the ceremony. Unless of course she's..." She rubbed her tummy and winked.

Faith couldn't argue with the logic, so she set about opening the prosecco and pouring both herself and Steph a glass. They had a quick toast before Steph excused herself to use the washroom. The moment she was gone, Faith turned to her sister and raised her eyebrows in question.

Hope laughed. "Hey, I've had a little bit of experience calming down frantic brides," she explained. "I'm definitely not new to it."

"A fact I'm super glad of. She does seem a little on edge

with it all. Maybe it was a bad idea to do it so quickly after Dax got back? I mean, they haven't even seen each other for a month."

"Not your call, sis. I know we've gotten to know her and she's our friend, but she's also a client and you don't get to make those types of decisions. You need to know where the line is."

Faith thought about it for a minute. She also thought about the information Logan had shared with her about Dax. Where *was* the line? And where should she be on it? The wedding planner side? Or the friend side?

If it were her...

The idea made her laugh out loud. It wouldn't be her. Not now. She couldn't think about Logan.

"Hello? Faith?"

She blinked hard and looked back at her sister, who was waving her hand and laughing at her. "I'm here. I'm listening."

"You were thinking about Logan?"

"What?" She crossed her arms and turned away. "No. I was not. Why would you say that?"

Hope only laughed. "You were too."

What kind of freaky twin thing was going on?

"I was *not.*" She spun on her sister and barked the words. "Why would you even say that?"

"Just a guess." Hope looked quite pleased with herself, which only pissed Faith off even more. "Because the two of you have been extra weird the last few days, and I just assumed that after we spoke about...well...what happened to giving it a chance?"

"Giving what a chance?"

Both sisters turned at the sound of Steph's voice. She'd curled her red hair into soft waves that she'd pinned up on her head in a casual, yet elegant updo. She was holding a beaded hairpiece in her hand and staring at them both with suspicious eyes. "What's going on?"

Faith sighed and, tired of the lie, opened her mouth to tell Steph the truth once and for all when her cell phone rang.

Logan.

There were a million reasons she didn't want to talk to him. But one very important reason she needed to. She held up a finger to the ladies and took the call.

"What's going on with the license?"

"Hello to you, too."

She bristled. "We're running out of time." Faith turned away from the other women, not wanting to worry Steph, but it was too late; she'd stepped closer and was clearly listening to the conversation. "What's going on?"

On the other end of the line, Logan sighed. "The dates are wrong," he said after a moment. "I don't know how to explain it, but the registry said there isn't a Stephanie Straub born on September 28, 1991 in the system. She doesn't exist."

"That doesn't make any sense." Faith shook her head and turned around. "Did you ever legally change your name to Starz?"

Steph shook her head. "No. It's just a stage name. My legal name is still Straub. At least until I take—"

Faith stopped listening. "That doesn't make sense," she said again to Logan on the line. "She didn't change her name. It should all work."

"What's the issue?" Hope asked from her seat. "The dates are wrong?"

Faith nodded. "I just don't—"

"I'll look into it." Hope grinned. "I have an idea."

"What—"

"Don't worry about it yet," Hope interrupted as she got up. "I think I have a plan. I need to make a call." She stopped by

Faith and whispered into her ear. "Keep her calm and don't worry. I'll let you know as soon as I know something."

There was nothing else to do but nod and smile and when Hope made her exit, Faith turned once more to Steph. "How about a top-up on that prosecco?"

"No license?" Stephanie drank from the glass Faith had just refilled. "What does that mean? I can't get married without a license, can I?"

"Let's not worry about it yet, okay? It's probably just a glitch at the registry. Sometimes computers make mistakes."

Faith sounded confident, but Stephanie wasn't an idiot.

"Maybe it's a sign." She sat down hard on the edge of the mattress. "Maybe I'm trying to do it too quickly. Everything is…" She turned to look at Faith. "Do you think Dax is the one for me?"

The other woman's face flickered with something Steph couldn't decipher, although she was pretty sure she'd seen the very same look in her new friend's face a few times already since Dax had arrived.

In fact, the entire feeling in the house had shifted when Dax got there the night before. Everyone seemed a little on edge and even Dax hadn't seemed…normal. Maybe she'd just never noticed it before, but Dax didn't seem quite as attentive as she remembered him. In fact, he seemed a little on the fringes of things. As if he couldn't—or wouldn't—fully engage.

When Faith still hadn't answered her question, Stephanie looked up from her lap at her new friend. "Well? Do you?"

Faith pressed her lips together and took a deep breath.

That didn't look promising.

Suddenly Steph knew she didn't want to hear Faith's

answer, but she couldn't seem to stop herself from pushing the other woman.

"Faith?"

"I think the better question is, do *you* think he's the one for you?"

"That's a cop-out." Steph dropped her head again. It may be a cop-out, but it was also a question she didn't want to answer herself. "Tell me the truth. Do you see the same thing with Dax and me that Hope and Levi have? That you and Logan have?"

Faith leaned against the dresser across the room. "You don't have to go through with it, Stephanie. If you're having any kind of doubts or second thoughts, or…well, anything. There's nothing saying that you have to do this. Not today," she added. "We're not going anywhere and if you want to have your wedding here another time, maybe after you've worked out whatever it is that's bothering you, I'm here for you. Totally. I just don't want you to rush into anything you're not ready for."

"But…" Stephanie twirled the ring on her finger, trying to remember the moment Dax had given it to her. She'd always wanted a small, quiet proposal. Something intimate, with just the two of them. But Dax had gotten down on one knee on the red carpet at the premiere of her last movie. It had been anything but quiet and intimate. And in hindsight, the proposal had taken all the attention off her, the star of the movie, and had put it all on him. And it hadn't been the first time something like that had happened. More than once, Dax had worked to earn more attention than her.

She'd never really paid it much mind before, because frankly, Steph didn't love the limelight. But when she stopped to think about it…

"Dax wanted the big wedding," she told Faith. "It was his

idea to get the press involved and turn it into a huge event. He even wanted to shop it around for a network special."

Faith snorted but quickly covered it with a cough.

"I think I thought that maybe by insisting on a super small wedding, it would be…" Tears pricked her eyes, but she blinked hard, unwilling to cry.

"It still will be beautiful, Steph. If this is what you want."

"Was this what it was like for Hope and Levi?"

Faith laughed. "Not even close. But that's only because those two are as stubborn as the day is long and were both so pig-headed that they almost lost each other. Also, the fact that they'd loved each other since they were kids played a role in their story. Totally different."

"Like you and Logan?" Steph loved hearing their stories. The love that the two sisters had found with their men was inspiring. It really was rare and it gave her hope. That was the whole reason she was at Ever After in the first place. It was good luck. Identical twins falling madly in love with cousins who had loved them their whole lives? It was better than a movie. No romcom could compete with that story line.

She waited for Faith to fill her with hope once again. But instead, Faith made a noise that was part sigh and part groan before she sat down hard on the mattress next to her. "I need to tell you something."

Steph swallowed hard against the lump in her throat. Every cell in her body was telling her to run away and not let Faith tell her whatever it was she was going to say. Probably that Dax was having an affair with his costar. That she'd overheard something. That Dax had told Logan and Levi the truth, that—

"Logan and I aren't together."

"What?" Steph's head snapped up. She screwed her face up and she shook her head because she clearly hadn't heard right. "You're not together?"

Faith shook her head softly. "No. It was a...well...it was all made up. We're not a couple."

Of course they were a couple. She'd seen them together. She'd seen them kiss and cuddle and...they went to bed together every night. Hell, she was almost sure she'd overheard them making love a few nights ago, but the look on Faith's face said differently.

"But you—"

"No." She cut her off. "It was an act." Something in her voice was sad. Regretful, almost, and maybe if there hadn't been so much weight to what she was saying, Stephanie might have actually felt bad for Faith, or asked her to explain herself and what she was feeling. Because there seemed to be a whole lot more to the story than what Faith was saying.

Especially because she'd seen the way Logan and Faith were with each other. She'd seen the way they *looked* at each other. The way they *touched* each other. That wasn't acting. She'd been around the best actors in the world and not even they could pull off the love that Faith and Logan seemed to have with each other.

There had to be more to what she was saying. It couldn't possibly be that simple. But...then again...maybe it was. Maybe, it wasn't enough to be true just because she wanted it to be. Maybe the woman she'd thought was a friend, and possibly even a *sister,* had just fed her a bunch of bullshit. But why? Why would Faith tell her such deep and twisted lies?

She knew exactly why.

"You just wanted to have the wedding, didn't you?" The moment she said it, Steph knew it was true. Just like everyone else in her life, Faith only wanted something from her. "You wanted to make the news. Host the wedding of the century." She shook her head. "I should have known."

"It wasn't like that, Steph."

But she didn't want to hear it. None of it.

She'd been here before. She'd dealt with people like Faith before.

She pushed herself up from the bed and walked to the mirror. She would not cry. She would not show this woman, whom up until a minute ago she'd thought was a friend, break her. Not like all the others before her.

No way.

She examined herself carefully in the mirror, trying to decide what to do while Faith kept talking.

"It really wasn't like that, Steph. I mean, it started out... well...it wasn't supposed to be...I really like you, Steph. You need to believe that. We didn't want to hurt you. We weren't trying to lie to you or—"

"Enough." Stephanie spun around. "I don't want to hear it." She shook her head, again willing the emotion to stay away. She would not cry in front of this woman who only a few days ago she'd actually hoped to be her sister.

What a fool she'd been.

"I'm getting married. And you are going to make it happen."

"But the license—"

"Then we'll do it without the license," she snapped. "Nothing is going to stop this wedding from happening. It's your *job.*"

Faith stood and shook her head as she walked toward her.

But the last thing Steph wanted was for her to get closer. "I mean it, Faith. I came here for you to be my wedding coordinator and that's what you are." She didn't need to say the words she meant. *It's all that you are.* "Please help me with my dress."

Faith looked as if she were about to argue again, but finally she pressed her lips together and nodded. "If that's what you want."

It wasn't what she wanted.

Or was it?

Maybe it was everything she'd ever wanted.

The problem was…she just didn't know anymore.

There was nothing to be done about the marriage certificate. After a few hours dealing with the registry, and multiple phone calls back and forth with Hope, they'd finally gotten to the bottom of why Stephanie's identification didn't match up to the information in the registry. But even with the proper details, they still couldn't finalize a marriage license.

And that was a problem.

Probably the biggest problem of the day, despite the information Logan now had in his possession. And it would have to wait.

Because Stephanie was less than thirty minutes from her wedding ceremony. The same ceremony that, Hope had just informed him, she was determined to go through with despite not having a license. It wouldn't be legal, but that was a detail she didn't seem to be too concerned about.

Which was probably a good thing, as far as Logan was concerned. If Stephanie insisted on marrying the jackass, at the very least, it wouldn't be legal. Which just made the entire thing seem even more ridiculous because Stephanie Starz—or Straub or whatever her last name was—was an amazing person. One he'd come to care for as a friend. And Dax Combs was probably the biggest idiot on earth if he didn't see how great she was, and what a jackass he was being about that whole thing.

He couldn't even be in the same room with Dax, which was why he'd sent Levi back to the ranch to deal with him. Logan wasn't a violent person, but the more time he spent with the narcissistic actor, the more he wanted to punch him in the face and that probably wouldn't go over very well with...well, everyone else.

As he made his way back to the ranch and the union he was certain would be doomed, Logan couldn't help but compare himself and Faith to Dax and Stephanie. Even though they were pretending to be a couple, they were better suited. He would never treat Faith the way Dax treated Steph. He would never pretend to...

Fuck.

That was the whole problem. He hadn't been pretending with her. Not ever. It had always been real for him. Even if Faith didn't believe it. And she didn't believe it. She was convinced that he'd been full of shit.

And *that* was the problem.

He pulled over on the side of the road and hit the steering wheel with the palm of his hand. He'd been such an idiot. *Why had he made the bet?* Of course she didn't believe that his feelings were real. Instead of just coming out and telling her like a real man, he'd been a big chicken shit and hidden behind a stupid bet, of all things.

Why?

Because he was scared.

It was simple. He was terrified that the woman he'd loved his entire life would reject him and for real this time. If he put his feelings out there honestly instead of teasing, and she *still* rejected him, then what was left?

He would never know if he didn't try.

If pretending to be with Faith was all he'd ever have, that would have to be enough. Especially because Logan knew in his heart that it hadn't been pretend at all. The last few weeks had been more real than anything he'd ever felt.

And he needed to make her understand that, because there was no one else for him. There never had been, and there never would be. He'd been a moron and maybe it was already too late. Maybe he'd already blown his chance with her.

But at least he was going to try.

He put the truck into gear and pulled out onto the highway again.

And maybe, at the same time, he could stop Stephanie from making the worst decision of her life. Because legal or not, marrying Dax would be a terrible thing and she deserved so much more. Especially now that he knew the truth.

Chapter Nineteen

HE WAS TOO LATE.

The wedding ceremony had already started by the time Logan pulled up in the yard. But that didn't mean he wasn't going to try to do what he could. He drove as close as he could get and then ran the rest of the way through the trees to the site they used for ceremonies. It was a beautiful spot by the river, and although it wasn't his favorite spot, it really was gorgeous.

Thankfully, there were only a handful of people in the clearing. The officiant, Dee, stood under the arch with Stephanie and Dax in front of her. He couldn't see Stephanie's face as she stared straight forward. Dax, on the other hand, looked around, smiling a huge toothy grin in every direction the photographer moved. Clearly, it was all just a big photo shoot for him. *Publicity. That's all it was.*

Seeing it made Logan even angrier.

He forced himself to look to Hope, who sat in a wheelchair, a small smile on her face while Levi stood behind her. Across from them was Faith. She looked gorgeous. And sad. *Really* sad.

Was it because of him? Or maybe it was because she was

watching Stephanie make a mistake? Did she believe him about Dax after all? *Yes.* Logan could tell by the press of her lips and the way she looked at the movie star, slightly on guard, suspicious, and tense all through her spine, that she did. Faith was never very good at hiding how she felt.

It was one of the things he loved about her.

Loved?

Yes. *Loved.*

He stood there for a moment, lost in the idea that yes, he loved Faith. He'd always loved her. It was more than just *feelings.* It was more than lust. It was definitely love. A year ago— hell, a month ago—if someone would have told him he'd be madly in love with the woman and not even remotely scared by the prospect of it, he would have laughed and run in the opposite direction.

But now, all he wanted to do was move toward her.

At the front of the clearing, Dee had obviously said something important, because everyone shifted and Steph and Dax turned a little to face each other.

Shit.

The wedding. The wedding he couldn't in good conscience let happen.

Dax took Stephanie's hand, and even from the distance he was at, Logan could see the smirk on his face. *How could Stephanie not see it? How could she settle for anything that wasn't everything?*

"No!" he yelled before he could stop himself. "Don't do it."

Everyone spun around. As he ran toward the couple, Logan had the thought that maybe there might have been a better way to do what he was about to do, but it was too late. He was committed.

"Stop!" He pushed himself directly between the bride and groom-to-be. "Don't do it, Steph."

Faith grabbed his arm and yanked him back toward her. "What are you doing?" she hissed in his ear. "Stop this."

"No." He looked her in the eyes and tried to wordlessly apologize for what he was about to do. "I'm sorry, Faith. I can't not say something."

Before she could object again, he turned to Stephanie, who looked absolutely stunning despite the daggers she was shooting from her eyes in his direction. "Steph, I'm so sorry to do this to you. I know how excited you were for this day and—"

"Logan." Levi appeared at his side and tried to put a hand on his shoulder, but Logan shrugged him off.

"He's not the man for you, Steph. You deserve much more than this. And I know I'm probably—"

"Are you seriously trying to pick up my fiancée right now?" Dax spun him around and confronted him.

Instead of being filled with rage the way Logan would have expected, Dax actually look pleased. His lips were flicked up in what could only be described as a smirk and his eyes twinkled. No doubt he was busy thinking about the great story that would come from Logan's outburst.

Especially if he was trying to twist it.

"No." Logan shook his head. "I'm not trying to pick up your fiancée." He turned to the woman who'd become his friend over the last little while, and his heart broke at the look on her pretty face. "I'm so sorry, Steph." He took her hand. "I really am. But you only deserve the best. You deserve to have a man who absolutely adores you and would move heaven and earth for you. You deserve a man like—"

"You?" Her face twisted. The sadness was gone, replaced by anger and what could only be described as disgust. "You think I deserve someone like you, because you're such a perfect boyfriend to Faith? Because you love and adore her and the two of you are absolutely perfect? That's what you would have me believe?"

Her words were laced with venom and even before looking to see Faith's expression, Logan knew that Stephanie knew the truth. Or at least, she thought she did. But she didn't know the whole truth.

Not even close.

Faith shook her head, just a little. No doubt to stop him from what she thought he was about to say. But he wasn't going to be stopped. Not now.

"No." Logan shook his head. "Not a man like me. You deserve better than me." He looked at Faith and held her eyes. "You both do."

"Drop it, Logan." Stephanie's normally sweet, soft voice was hard and pointed. "I already know the truth," she continued. "Faith came clean. You're both liars. I know that now."

She knew?

One look at Faith, who gave him a quick nod, confirmed it.

"Well then," Logan turned back to Steph, "that just proves my point. You deserve better than a man who doesn't put you first. Who doesn't put you and your needs above everything else. You deserve someone who isn't just interested in the optics of a wedding or the media attention he can get for it."

"Wait a minute." Dax, who'd remained remarkably quiet up until now, stepped forward and pushed himself between Logan and his bride-to-be. "Who the fuck do you think you are, barging in here and stopping my wedding?" His words were tight, but Dax couldn't hide the gleam of excitement in his eyes. Clearly he wasn't as good of an actor as he thought he was. "And what's this about lying? Who's lying?"

"They are."

"We can explain."

"No one."

Everyone spoke at once, but it was Faith who took charge.

Enough was enough.

Faith couldn't stand there for one more minute and let this train wreck of a wedding continue. Logan had already completely committed career suicide for Ever After. No doubt Dax Combs would have this little scandal all over the media and tabloids by the end of the day. No one would ever want to book Ever After for their wedding ever again. They would be blacklisted.

But that wasn't even the worst part of it all.

Judging by Stephanie's face, she was either going to burst into tears or start hitting Logan, or both. And it had to stop.

"We're lying." Faith took a step forward. "Logan and I have been lying from the start. We're not a couple." She turned to Logan. "I already told her the truth. It didn't matter."

"It did matter!" Tears streaked down Stephanie's face. "Of course it mattered. You lied to me and made me believe a story that wasn't true. A story that I bought into and believed with my heart. You made me believe in the magic, that maybe if I married Dax here, some of it would rub off on us and we could be happy too. Because we don't have what you all have." She spun in a circle to encompass Levi and Hope as well as Faith and Logan, who now stood next to each other, helplessly looking on.

"We never did," she said, her voice softer as she turned to Dax. "We never had anything close to what they all have. Made up or not." She lifted her bouquet before dropping it helplessly to her side. "Even if it's fake, it's still stronger than what we have." Tears flowed freely down her cheeks now. "I just wanted it so badly. I just thought maybe...just maybe I could have a little piece of this magic."

Magic.

That word again. Stephanie may be ridiculously angry

with her, but it still didn't change the fact that she was her friend. She might be mad now but it wouldn't last forever, and no way was Faith going to sit by and let her believe that she couldn't have that magic. Because she could.

"Steph?"

Slowly, the other woman turned around to face her.

"There is magic here." She spoke quickly before she could be stopped. "And maybe it's not the way you thought, with the identical twins each finding their happily ever afters." She shook off the hurt in her heart just speaking the words aloud caused and kept going. "But there's a different kind of magic here. A magic that sometimes brings you together with the one person you are meant to be with since you were kids." She turned to smile at Hope and Levi before continuing. "The magic that helps you find love again after you thought all hope was lost." She thought to Brody and Sarah, who'd been through so much. "And the kind of magic that helps you see your best friend is so much more than that." She referred to Damon and Katie. "And that's magic, Stephanie. Maybe the magic of Ever After can't turn a relationship into something it's not. But maybe you can——"

"Realize that you deserve more," Logan interjected.

She shot him a look, but he put his hand on her arm and squeezed gently as he continued talking.

"Maybe the magic of Ever After looks different for you because what you needed to learn was that you deserve and are worthy of so much more. That your true love hasn't been discovered yet."

Stephanie sniffled and dabbed at her eyes, but she was listening. She was no longer yelling. In fact, everyone was listening, including Faith, who couldn't believe that such things were coming out of the mouth of the wisecracking pain in her ass. She tried not to stare at him open-mouthed as Logan turned to her now and spoke.

"Maybe the magic of this place is in finally seeing what has been in front of you all this time for what it really is."

What the hell was he—

"I love you, Faith."

What?

"I know now that I've always loved you. I've just been too stupid to see it for what it really is, and then too proud to expose myself to you so completely."

"Logan. You don't have to do this." Faith shook her head. She needed to stop this. She needed to stop *him*. It was bad enough he'd completely destroyed this wedding and, along with it, their reputation. He did not need to make a fool of her in the process. "They already know the truth. Don't make it worse."

"Worse?" He chuckled, but shook his head and grabbed both her hands in his. "The only way I can make this worse now is if I walk away from here and you still don't believe me when I tell you exactly how I feel. I was never acting, Faith. Ever."

No.

It was too much. He couldn't be saying what she thought he was saying. And even if he was…Faith turned to her sister, who had been sitting quietly in her wheelchair the whole time. She was grinning, and if Faith wasn't mistaken, there looked to be a tear in her eye.

Not helpful.

She turned to look at Stephanie, who, up until a few hours ago, she might have considered an ally in this entire situation. To her surprise, Steph no longer looked angry, and she was watching the proceedings with a very strange look on her face that she couldn't decipher.

"Look at me, Faith." Logan squeezed her hands gently until she turned around again. "I'm not saying this because of a bet. Or to get the wedding of the century. Or for any other reason than the most important one. I love you."

It wasn't a bet? It wasn't…it was real?

It took her a minute, and then another to let his words register, but Logan didn't rush her. She looked down at their clasped hands and let the heat from his body flow into hers. The meaning of his words hit her the way they were supposed to and then, finally, she looked up.

"You *love* me?"

His smile lit up his entire face. His eyes sparkled and he didn't even hesitate as he said, "So much that it hurts to be near you and not have you understand exactly how I feel. Earlier, when you told me you were done…" He shook his head and swallowed hard. "I won't accept that, Faith. You and I…we're so far from done. We're only just beginning."

Faith struggled to process what he was saying.

Was it just another attempt to get to her or pull one over on her?

He'd done it before. He'd teased her and fooled her *so* many times in the past. Was this time different?

And how could she know?

Faith didn't speak, but watched Logan carefully. He looked straight at her, his gaze never wavering. The smile on his face was true, not cocky or teasing or arrogant, but…genuine.

"You love me?" she asked again. Something inside her needed to hear it again.

"I. Love. You." He shook her hands a little and brought them to his lips. "And I always will. You can push and push, but I'm not budging. I love you today, and always, Faith Turner. We were meant for each other, and I know you believe that, too."

She did. And it wasn't just because she wanted to. It wasn't just because she loved *him.* She felt it in her heart. The very same heart that had been so closed off for so long that she'd missed her own true feelings for too many years.

Dammit. Hope was right.

And thank God she was.

Without wasting another second, Faith pulled her hands out of his so she could wrap them around him, pull him close, and kiss him harder than she ever had before.

No one else mattered. Nothing else mattered.

Once her lips were on his and he was kissing her back with just as much need, the entire world was right.

It wasn't until someone behind them muttered, "It's about time," that they pulled apart.

Logan kept his arm around her as they turned to face the small crowd they'd managed to forget about.

As soon as Faith's gaze landed on Stephanie, the smile slipped from her face again. "Steph, I'm—"

Chapter Twenty

"DON'T SAY IT." Stephanie held up her hand. If she heard one more person apologize, she thought she might straight up lose her mind. "Just…leave it."

"Leave it?" It was Dax interjecting now. "What the hell do you mean, *leave it?* We're supposed to be getting married, Steph."

She couldn't decide whether Dax sounded pissed off about the interrupted nuptials, happy about them, or sad. His voice, face, and body language were all telling her different things. And for the first time since she'd met him, she looked at him through different eyes.

Faith and Logan had been right about him. Dax Combs wasn't her forever.

Hell. He wasn't even her right now.

He was an actor, and she couldn't help but feel as though he'd been acting the entire time they'd been together.

"You don't want this," she said softly. "Not for the right reasons."

"That's not—"

"It is." She shook her head. "Besides, even if you did...I don't."

Saying it out loud for the first time felt like a weight around her neck had been lifted. She could make it to the surface and finally breathe again.

"I do want it, Stephanie." He grabbed her hand. "Let's just do it. Think of the press. It'll be—"

"The press." She pulled her hand away. "That's what it's always been about, right? The press." She nodded softly as it all clicked into place. "I can't believe I fell for it."

"You fell for *me*, Stephanie." Dax grabbed her hand and dropped to one knee. "And I fell for you. That flutter in your belly every time we're together—I have it, too. It's more than just nerves; it's—"

"A line from your next movie." Again, she pulled her hand away from him. This time she laughed. "Are you seriously reciting *lines* to me?"

"It's not a—"

"It is." She laughed harder. "I remember reading that script. Remember? I turned it down." It was true. Her agent had presented the script to her, but Stephanie found it thin and vapid, and passed. As did their first and second choice for the male lead, if she remembered correctly, so they'd offered it to Dax. Despite the fact that he behaved as if he'd been their first choice, walking around like hot shit.

All of it made her want to howl with laughter while at the same time, bursting into tears. "I can't believe you would try to use lines on me. And worse, that I believed them." She looked down at the dress that only a few hours earlier she'd thought was the most beautiful gown in the world. Now, even it seemed tarnished. Nothing had been right from the start. She'd wanted it to be, so badly that she'd ignored all the signs. Including the marriage certificate.

"We couldn't get married anyway," she said to Dax. "We don't even have a legal marriage certificate."

It was his turn to look surprised but before he could ask about it, Hope spoke up.

"Actually, Steph? About that. I have your mom on the phone."

"My mom?"

Hope nodded shyly. "Sorry it's taken so long, but she was harder to track down than I would have thought. I had a suspicion about things, but it wasn't until I spoke with her and then Logan confirmed it at the registry earlier...." She held up her cell phone lamely. "Anyway... I think you should talk to her."

Stephanie took the cell phone gingerly and, with her bouquet still in one hand, held it to her ear as she walked a few paces away from the group. "Mom?"

"Honey. You're getting married? I had...well, I guess I did know. I saw it in the...oh, Stephanie. I'm so sorry."

The tears that had been on the verge all day finally spilled over. "No, Mom. It's me who's sorry. I don't know why I didn't tell you."

That wasn't true. She knew very well why she hadn't said anything. Despite their differences, her mother would have seen right through Dax and would have told Steph exactly what she thought. And she hadn't wanted to hear it. "I'm so sorry, Mom. But it doesn't matter because I'm not getting married. Not now and not with..." She looked back at Dax, who'd pulled his cell phone out of his pocket—of course he had his phone with him—and was madly typing on it. "Not to Dax," she whispered. "It's not right. And I couldn't get a marriage license anyway. I don't know—"

"That's my fault."

"What? How could that possibly be your fault? I think the registry just had an—"

"I lied about your birthday."

175

Something in her mother's voice froze her to the spot. "You what?"

"You have every right to be mad. We never did it to be hurtful or to cause any issues for you." Her mother's words came hot and fast. "It was a spur-of-the-moment decision because I always felt like the day they put you in my arms for the first time, that was your birthday. That was the day that I came alive, that we became a family. That was the day that started everything. So it should be your birthday."

"But it wasn't my birthday?" Nothing made sense. Slowly, Stephanie regained the feeling in her feet and she turned around slowly to face the group, who were all still watching her. All but Dax, who was now talking on his phone and completely oblivious to the earth-shattering news that was just delivered to her. "What's my birthday, Mom?" She locked eyes with Hope. The smile on the other woman's face was unmistakable. And that's when she knew. "Mom?" she asked again, needing the clarification. "What day was I born?"

Her mother took a sharp intake of breath and then she said what Stephanie already knew in her heart. "September 2, 1991. You were born in Calgary. We adopted you a few weeks later and brought you home."

Hope nodded in response to her unasked question.

"So that means…"

"It could be true," her mother said. "I was talking to Hope. She's very lovely, by the way. And the information she has matches up with the very limited information that I have. It was a closed adoption, but we were always open to your birth mother reaching out. Apparently the flood years ago destroyed everything, so there wouldn't be much information for your birth mother by the time you turned eighteen and she could access it. But yes," she said slowly. "Everything else looks like it adds up. I would say…"

"Mom? Are you crying?" To Steph's surprise, tears fell

down her own cheeks as well. "Mom. You're always going to be my mom. You know that."

"I do," she said after a moment. "I've always been so scared that we weren't enough for you. That's why, I always... oh, Stephanie. Do you think you could come home for a visit?"

She didn't even hesitate. "As soon as I can."

Steph promised her mother she'd call and make plans as soon as was reasonable, and disconnected the call. For the first time in a long time, she was looking forward to visiting her parents. But first, she had a few other things to deal with.

She walked straight to Dax, who put his phone down as she approached. For everything he was, and everything he may have pretended to be, he was still her fiancé and despite it all, she knew he cared about her. "Dax?" She reached for his hand.

"This isn't happening, is it?"

Instead of saying no, she shrugged. "I don't even know who I am," she said softly. "How could I possibly get married?"

She couldn't be sure how much he'd overheard of her conversation, or even how much he'd even been paying attention, but he nodded. "I get that."

When she looked into his eyes, she could once again see the man she'd fallen in love with. The vulnerable, kind-hearted man who didn't put fame ahead of his heart. Somewhere along the line, things had changed a little. But not entirely. He was still in there.

"You know how much I care about you, don't you?"

"And I, you." She stood on her tippy-toes and pressed a kiss to his cheek. "Sometimes things just don't work out the way you planned."

He nodded and she knew he was trying not to look affected by what was happening. "Not right now, but maybe one day?"

Her smile was kind. "Maybe one day."

It surprised her that she wasn't as upset as she thought she might be as Dax turned and walked away. It would probably hit her later that he hadn't been the man she'd thought he was, but for the moment, she had the best consolation prize she could have imagined.

Stephanie turned to see Faith standing next to Hope in her wheelchair. Everyone else had disappeared. There was a lot they needed to talk about and those conversations weren't all going to be easy, that was for sure. But no matter how difficult it was going to be to wrap her head around where it was she came from, and the new family she had suddenly thrust upon her, it would be worth it. With so many unknowns, that was one constant. With tears in her eyes and a smile on her face, Stephanie picked up her skirts and went to give her sisters a big hug.

Chapter Twenty-One

THREE WEEKS LATER...

"This is crazy." Faith looked at her reflection in the mirror and then back at her sisters.

It still felt strange to think that she had more than one sister. A bigger family than she'd ever known and definitely one she'd never expected. Their relationship was still new, and it was going to take some work as they navigated this new normal. But now that Stephanie was back in town and taking a hiatus from work for a bit, they had time.

Hope and Stephanie wore matching grins that stretched across their faces as they spoke at the same time.

"Not crazy at all."

"Makes perfect sense to me."

Faith shook her head. "You're both nuts." She turned back to her reflection. "This is absolutely crazy," she said to herself before her own mouth split into a grin. "The best kind of crazy."

She was wearing a fitted golden gown with lace inlay and

the subtlest sequins sewn down the bodice. The fabric hugged her curves until it flared out at her knees to pool around her feet, with a train flowing behind her. It was incredibly girly and never in a million years did she ever expect she'd be wearing a dress like this. Never mind that she'd be wearing a dress as gorgeous as this on her wedding day.

Her wedding day.

It was so crazy, but three weeks ago after Logan's crazy declaration where Faith was finally able to admit her own feelings, they'd completely flown out like a tap that couldn't be shut off. In an instant, everything seemed right. The sky was a little bit bluer, the sun a little brighter. The bird's song was a little sweeter, and she was perfectly aware that she was a total cliché.

And she didn't care.

She'd waited way too long for the kind of happiness that loving Logan brought her and now that she had it, and they'd both been able to get over themselves so they could be with each other, Faith wanted to tell everyone she met about it. In a perfect piece of irony that wasn't lost on anyone, it turned out that Faith was the more romantic twin after all.

Which was how she'd ended up proposing to Logan. They'd been completely inseparable, and considering he was already living with her—for real now—it didn't make sense to wait any longer. Besides, they'd known each other practically all their lives and...when you know, you know.

Of course he'd said yes, which she'd expected since she was naked and straddling his body. Okay, maybe not the most romantic way to propose, but it got the job done and they both agreed to tie the knot as soon as possible.

Which was how she came to be standing in a wedding gown in front of a mirror, getting ready to marry the love of her life.

Because he was. Without a doubt, Logan was the love of her life and she couldn't wait to make it official.

"Who would have thought this would be happening, right?" Faith laughed and tucked a stray curl that had slipped out of her updo behind her ear.

"We did."

"Us."

Hope and Stephanie answered at the same time. They wore matching dresses in what Hope described as *champagne*. Hope's dress was cut a little looser than her sister's since her baby bump was beginning to make an appearance. Hope insisted it was too early to be showing but Faith secretly hoped an upcoming ultrasound would reveal that it was twins. She couldn't imagine anything better than having twin babies around. Especially if she got to be the auntie who spoiled them and then handed them back when they started to cry.

"No way did you think I was going to be a total wedding suck."

"Of course we knew." It was Steph who walked behind her and together they looked at their reflections in the mirror. Now that the shock of everything had worn off, and the DNA tests had proved that, in a crazy twist of fate, the world's biggest superstar celebrity, Stephanie Starz, was in fact their long-lost older sister, they could actually start to see the similarities in their appearances that had always been there. They had the same shape eyes, even if the color was different, and the same tiny nose. Stephanie's mouth was different; she definitely had fuller, more luscious lips that both of the twins envied. And of course there was the red curly hair, which was in fact natural. There still wasn't much known about Stephanie's birth father, but she was interested in discovering what she could. Out of interest more than anything. And now that she had the full support of her parents, as well as her new sisters, she finally had the courage to look into it.

In fact, Faith had noticed a lot of changes with Steph in the last few weeks. When she got back from visiting her parents, she seemed calmer and more sure of herself. Before, she'd always had a bit of an air of trying to impress and be something she wasn't, but that had changed. Almost as if knowing the truth had settled her in a way she hadn't realized she'd needed.

Either way, everything about finding Stephanie had been a good thing.

"Do you remember when I first came to town?" Stephanie said. "You tried to pretend it was all Hope who handled the wedding details, but it was you, too. I could see it in your eyes when you talked about the ceremonies and flowers and…all of it, really. You might not even know it, but you are and, as far as I know, have always been a total wedding suck."

"Well, not always." Hope laughed. "She definitely hated weddings for a while. I think Logan had a lot to do with her change of heart. It was all part of my master plan."

Faith shook her head with a groan as Hope tapped her fingers together like an evil villain.

Maybe it was all part of a greater plan, but Faith didn't care. As long as he was waiting for her at the end of the aisle, that was all that mattered.

Logan had never felt so calm and at peace as he waited at the end of the aisle.

Especially when it came to Faith.

For longer than he could remember, the woman had gotten under his skin, driven him crazy, and tested him in more ways than he ever could have invented.

And all of it had been perfect and totally worth it.

The moment the music started and she appeared from the

opening in the trees, everything was perfect.

She was perfect.

And absolutely gorgeous as she walked toward him. Faith had always been the most beautiful woman he'd ever seen, but wearing a wedding gown and a smile that was just for him, she was next level.

"Damn, woman," he whispered as she neared. "Are you trying to give me a heart attack before we even tie the knot? You look amazing." He didn't bother to hide his open appraisal of his wife-to-be. "Seriously, absolutely amazing."

She took his hand and squeezed. "You don't look too bad yourself. Who knew you cleaned up so well?"

All of their family and friends—who had all forgiven them for trying to lie about their relationship only a few weeks earlier, because obviously they had all seen the truth before they had—had joined them by the river for their ceremony. It wasn't the usual ceremony site, but another spot Logan had discovered weeks earlier, which happened to be a special spot of Faith's as well. He knew there was a reason he liked it.

A tiny meadow, with a rock outcropping on one side, there'd been no room for chairs next to the river that was moving slow so late in the season, but still bubbled over the rocks, providing the perfect background noise. Their guests circled them as Dee performed their ceremony that she'd written just for them.

Secretly, Logan was glad they were recording it because there was no way he was going to remember all of the details that had them laughing at times and crying at others.

But then it was finally their turn to say their vows. It was a moment Logan had been waiting for longer than he cared to admit. Some might say he was rough around the edges, and not a romantic, but he'd just spent the last few months surrounded by weddings. And the love of his life. He knew exactly what was to be said. But it was Faith's turn first.

"Logan, it hasn't always been easy with us." Faith started speaking. "But easy isn't any fun. Easy isn't exciting, and that's what makes us so perfect. Thank you for being the challenge I've always needed, the support I never knew I needed, and the safe place I'll always need. I vow to support you and love you for the rest of my life."

Logan reached out and wiped a tear from her cheek. He never thought he'd see the day that Faith Turner would be standing before him, reciting vows with a tear in her eye. But damn, was he ever glad that day was here.

"Faith," he began. "I have loved you my entire life. It just took me a little bit to figure it out." A titter of laughter went up among their guests. "But now that I know it, I'll never let you go." He paused for a beat. "I vow to always keep you wild. To challenge you and fight for you every day. I promise to never make a bet with you again, unless there's no chance either of us will lose." They both laughed. "Because as long as I have you, I win. We both win."

"We do."

"Hey," Dee interjected with a laugh. "You're skipping ahead."

"We always do," Logan said as seriously as he could before looking at Faith once again and squeezing her hand in his. "And last but not least, I vow to cash in my prize from our very first bet, every single night for the rest of my life." Her face went red the way he knew it would but because no one else knew the terms of their bet, it was perfect. He blew her a kiss and she shook her head with a laugh.

"I wouldn't expect or accept anything less."

Dee completed the rest of the ceremony, they finished with a kiss that was only a teaser for what would happen later that night, and their friends and family broke into a cheer before closing the circle into a tight group hug.

"Pretty wild summer, hey?" Levi put a beer in front of him hours later, at their reception dance. Faith was out on the dance floor with a circle of women around her, throwing up her arms in a *Grease* medley. And as much as Logan liked to dance with her, *Grease* was one he would happily sit out.

He lifted the beer in gratitude. "It was definitely one for the books." He took a large swallow. "But I wouldn't change a thing."

"Me neither." Levi lifted his beer. "Except, of course, for Hope being sick. But…"

"She's going to be fine."

"She is. And the baby." Levi shook his head in wonder. "Who would have thought we'd be sitting here like this when I came back to town a few months ago? Crazy."

"What's crazy?" The men turned to see Damon, Nick, Brody, and Jeremy join them.

"All of it." Logan shrugged.

They seemed to accept that answer and everyone lifted their drink in a cheers of solidarity.

"Well," Nick said when they'd finished the toast. "I like the kind of crazy you guys have around here. I've been thinking of sticking around."

Logan followed his gaze to the dance floor and a very specific redhead. "Your decision wouldn't have anything to do with my sister-in-law, now would it?"

"Hard to say." He winked at Logan.

But it was a problem for a different night. Besides, Stephanie could hold her own. Of that much he was certain.

They broke into chatter and laughter, taking turns ribbing one another the way only good friends can, which was why nobody noticed when the woman approached the barn door they were sitting next to. They didn't notice as she knocked, which was futile considering the music was so loud anyway. And they didn't notice when she walked straight up to their table. They, in fact, didn't notice her until she cleared her throat right as the DJ was changing the song. In the musical lull, the woman's voice rang out—and everyone noticed.

"Excuse me," she said, somewhat timid now that everyone in the room was looking at her. "I was told I could find you here." She shifted a bundle she held against her chest. Something else no one had noticed. A baby.

She looked directly at the table of men, but Logan couldn't make out who she was looking at specifically, which was what made everything even a little more crazy when she said, "I have something for you."

I hope you enjoyed Faith and Logan's happily ever after. It was a long time coming, but the best thing are worth waiting for, right?
I hope you think so because there will be more stories of love in the Ever After Series coming soon because there are a lot more residents of Glacier Falls who still need to find love.
Who do you think will be first?

Make sure to sign up for my newsletter so you'll be the first to hear when a new story is released!
You can join me here —>
https://elenaaitken.com/newsletter/

In the meantime, if you love small town romances, you'll love my series, The McCormicks. And you can download the first in the series for FREE!
Read on for a preview of Love in the Moment!

Love in the Moment

Ian McCormick stole a glance at the woman sitting next to him. He'd picked her up only ten minutes earlier from the bus station and already he'd run out of things to talk about. In fact, beyond the general introductions they'd exchanged, they really hadn't spoken at all. He felt as if he should say something to break the silence, but every time he opened his mouth, he drew a blank. What was he supposed to say to the younger half-sister he'd never met?

The sister that he'd never had any desire to meet, not since finding out about her existence almost ten years ago. As far as he was concerned, Ian could have gone the rest of his life without knowing about Chelsea or her sister, Amber's existence. And he really didn't see any need to get to know either of them. After all, they were the reason his entire life had imploded all those years ago.

Okay, that wasn't entirely fair. It wasn't their fault that their father had led a secret life, with a completely different family. A family he'd finally left his *other* family for, leaving Ian, his brothers, and his mother all alone. *No. It wasn't the girls' fault.* But all of the reasoning in the world hadn't made it any easier for Ian to wrap his head around it. Despite the fact that it had been almost a decade ago.

He snuck another look at the girl who had barely looked up from her phone since she'd sat down in the jeep. There was definitely a family resemblance. She had their father's green eyes, just like he did. And the dark, thick hair. He hated to admit it, but there was no denying she was his sister. And it wasn't as if he could spend the whole summer not talking to her. He'd made a promise to Declan, his second youngest brother.

"It's not her fault," Declan had said on the phone. *"Chelsea and Amber aren't to blame, Ian. You need to get over it."*

Dec was right. He did need to get over it, especially since she was going to be staying with him all summer. He took a breath and opened his mouth to say something, but didn't have a chance.

"I know you hate me."

Ian shut his mouth dumbly.

"And I suppose you think you have a reason to," Chelsea continued. "But it wasn't my idea to come here, you know? Declan pretty much insisted that it would be *good for me* or something, and…well…I kinda trust Dec. Besides, I didn't really have anywhere else to go."

He swallowed hard, giving himself a moment. "I don't hate you." As he spoke the words, he realized they were true. "I just don't know you. And Declan's right. It will be good for you here."

"You don't even know why he said that."

"I don't need to." Ian slowed the jeep to take the turn that would lead them out of town, toward the cottages. His house sat at the end of a row of other log cabins that were used primarily by summer people. Most of the houses were built by families who came from the city for the summer months, and they were still locked up tight because the season wouldn't start for another month or so. It was quiet, but Ian liked it. At least for now, while he was getting settled. And it was true, he didn't know why Declan thought it was a good idea for Chelsea to get out of the city for the summer, but he had a few guesses, and there was no doubt that a little bit of quiet would be good for her, too. "I trust Declan, too," he said as the jeep bumped over the dirt road. It was impossible not to trust Declan. Out of all of his siblings, Dec was definitely the most trustworthy, and the most compassionate and caring and...he was pretty much everything good in the world. "If he thinks it'll be good for you out here, he's probably right."

She shrugged and turned back to her cell phone, looking up a moment later in horror. "The service is terrible here."

"One of my favorite features." He smiled.

"Why would that be a good thing?"

He ignored the question. "It's not that bad, really. Just a little spotty sometimes. Besides, you'll be able to get Wi-Fi at the Dockside as soon as I get it hooked up."

"The Dockside?"

"The new marina." Ian couldn't help but smile. "Cool name, right?" The main reason he'd returned to Cedar Springs was because the economy was starting to pick up, and there were business opportunities to be had. One of the first he'd found was the old marina. It was just next to the Grizzly Paw on the beach in town and Ian remembered it as *the* meeting place for summer fun. He picked it up for a bargain basement price, probably because it needed so much work. By the looks of things, it had sat empty for years and it would definitely take a little elbow grease to get it up and running again. Not that

Ian was afraid of hard work. In fact, that had always been his favorite part of a new business: turning nothing into something. "I just closed on it yesterday. And with any luck, it will be open and ready for business in time for the season to start. But if that's going to happen, I'm going to need a little help."

She looked at him sideways. "And I suppose you want me to help."

"You got it. Call it…the price of admission."

She rolled her eyes and shoved her phone into her duffel bag. "Why not? I guess a summer job won't hurt."

"Oh no." Ian braced himself for her response to what he was about to tell her. "Helping at the marina isn't a summer job—it's just an expectation. I got you a job, too. You'll be starting at the Grizzly Paw right away. Sam's an old friend of mine, and she's doing me a favor by giving you this job, so I know you won't let me down."

"Two jobs?"

"No." He shook his head. "Just one. And a family project."

"But I'm never going to have any time to have fun," she wailed.

That was the point, at least as far as Ian was concerned. He didn't know much about twenty-two-year-old girls, but from what Declan had told him, Chelsea was making far too many poor choices. And as the big brother—whether he wanted to be or not—it was going to be his job to help her make good ones. Or keep her too busy to make anything but.

When Gwen Henderson had dreamed of her triumphant return to Cedar Springs after years of hard work and sacrifice, she'd dreamed of driving an expensive convertible down Main Street, her dark hair floating in the breeze as all the men's heads turned to see the beautiful and famous celebrity she'd turned out to be as they kicked themselves for not dating her when they had their chance.

Yes, in her fantasies, it was perfect. In reality, however, she had not imagined that on the eve of her summer visit to Cedar Springs, her secondhand Mustang would have some random, and likely expensive, engine problem that would require her taking the bus into town. And she most certainly did not expect that the one man who'd not only turned her down as a teenager, but had publicly humiliated her ten years earlier at the Summer Equinox Festival, would be there when she got off the bus.

Ian McCormick.

He didn't even *live* in Cedar Springs. What were the odds the one man who still haunted—no, not haunted...*visited*—her dreams would not only be standing there when she got off the stupid, humiliating bus, but would also look her square in the eye and not even recognize her?

If she was honest with herself, and she'd made that a habit over the last few years, that was the part that hurt the most. Ian McCormick had been her biggest teenage crush. No, her *only* teenage crush. Every summer for four years, she had lusted after him. Practically threw herself at him that final summer. But he'd barely even noticed her and when she thought she'd finally had a date with him at the festival, he'd stood her up. Left her there all alone. She knew now he'd only said yes to the date out of pity. After all, it didn't make sense for someone as handsome and smart as Ian McCormick to go out with fat, pimple-faced, four-eyed, frizzy-haired *Giant Gigi*. At the time, she'd been heartbroken—totally destroyed, really. But time and distance had taught her social order. The other thing time and distance had taught her was the impact that health, fitness, contacts, clear skin, a new hair-do, and a name change could do for social order.

It had been five years since she'd dropped the stupid childhood nickname, adopted a fitness regime and lost seventy-five pounds, finding herself and a new career in the process. Early on in her transformation, Gwen decided to document everything on social media, using a blog and then a Facebook and Instagram account to chronicle her progress. The result was not only a whole new body, but also a very loyal following, commercial and marketing deals, and the potential for a book and maybe even a reality television show. She was a very different person than the sad, overweight teenager she'd been on her summer visits to see her grandma in Cedar Springs. *Very* different. And with women looking up to her and men lining up to date her, she no longer needed Ian McCormick to validate her worth.

But if that was true, why had her heart done a stupid little flip when he'd grabbed her bag at the bus stop? And why had her pulse raced out of control when he looked at her? How was it even possible that he could still have that effect on her after all these years?

"Gwen!"

Deanna Gordon shot out of the building across the street and without even looking, raced across the street and pulled her into a hug. "Oh my goodness, you look amazing." Deanna held her out at arm's length for a fraction of a second before she pulled her back into a hug. "I'm so glad you're finally here. I was going to meet you at the bus stop—that's crazy that your car broke down—but I got caught up with a patient and—"

"It's okay." Gwen finally cut her off with a laugh. "I literally only walked half a block. Don't worry about it."

Deanna bent down and scooped up her bag. "Is this all you have? One duffel bag? I don't think I could travel that light if I tried."

Gwen laughed again. "Are you kidding? The rest of my bags are coming later. I may have sweet-talked the guy at the depot to deliver them personally."

"You did not?"

She only smiled in response. It wasn't often that Gwen used her curves and killer smile to get her way, but sometimes she couldn't seem to help herself. Besides, it's not as though she did it very often.

Deanna shook her head, but her friend smiled. "Hey, if you can get away with it...why not, right?"

"Exactly. And heaven knows I haven't always had this skill. I might as well take advantage sometimes. But don't tell anyone, okay?"

Deanna stared at her. "Who would I tell?"

She forgot sometimes that not everyone lived their whole life online. For Gwen, it was normal to record everything, and censor anything she didn't want getting out. It was a carefully constructed existence, one that was almost entirely public, because she'd built her following by *not* keeping very much private. Her readers liked to hear everything about her, including her workouts, what she had for dinner, her dates, and even more personal things about her dating habits. Not that she'd had much to report lately. She may get a lot of attention from men, but that attention disappeared pretty quickly when they found out who she was and what she did for a living.

"Forget it." Gwen shrugged it off. "I didn't really mean it like that. I mean..."

"I keep forgetting what you do for a living," Deanna said. "I mean, it's crazy to me that you can do that for a *job*. Oh, but I didn't mean it like that. I'm sorry, Gwen. It's just—"

"It's fine. I totally get it. It is crazy. I'm not offended." She decided to change tact and confide in the one person who would totally understand. "But you know what *did* offend me?"

Her friend froze on the sidewalk and waited.

"Ian McCormick." She pronounced every syllable of his name with an edge.

"Ian? You saw him?"

"You know he's here?"

Deanna blinked at her mildly before she put a smile back on her face and ushered Gwen down the sidewalk. "You know what? Let's drop your bag off and then you can tell me all about it over a cup of coffee."

Gwen eyed her friend and shook her head. "How about a *drink*?"

"Why didn't you tell me Ian McCormick was here?" Gwen sat across from Deanna at her kitchen table, a glass of soda water in her hand. She'd gone for the soda, deciding against alcohol. It was her default drink, but now that she had it, she wished she'd gone for something stronger after all. *Ian McCormick was in Cedar Springs.* That had not been part of the plan. Not at all. Sure, whenever she thought of her summers in Cedar Springs visiting her grandma, Ian figured largely in her memory. Whether he knew it or not, his attention—or lack thereof, as was the case—had figured largely in her teenage life. She couldn't remember a summer she hadn't spent lusting after him. As one of the *summer* kids, he was kind of a celebrity among the local kids. Not that she'd been a local kid. But she also wasn't a summer kid. Gwen had definitely floated and never really had any friends except for Deanna.

Ian had no shortage of girls after him, but he'd never wanted to date any of them.

No. That wasn't true. He just hadn't wanted to date *her*. Not that she could blame him. If she'd been a teenage boy back then, *she* wouldn't have wanted to date her. Almost a hundred pounds overweight, with bad hair and glasses, she was a walking cliché. Hell, she was even more of a cliché now that she'd lost all the weight, turned her life around and was returning to her past childhood haunts. She was a made-for-TV movie, for goodness sake.

"I honestly didn't think it mattered." Deanna joined her at the table. "He's a summer kid."

"A...he's not a kid anymore. And, B...you know he's way more than that. He's *way more*."

Deanna almost spat out her water. "No."

"No what?"

"No way you still have a thing for Ian McCormick."

Gwen didn't even have to answer that question, because the woman she'd always considered to be her best friend knew her well enough to know the answer. Or, she should have known her better than that, anyway. She narrowed her eyes and tilted her head.

"No way." Deanna shook her head. "Gwen, how can you possibly still be hung up on him? Honestly, I thought maybe after...well..."

"We said we'd never talk about that, remember?"

The situation they were never to discuss was a moment that could have broken up their friendship forever, but the girls made a decision not to let it affect them. Even though it had been hard, very hard for Gwen. The last summer she'd come to visit, Ian had arrived earlier than he usually had and somehow, Deanna and Ian ended up together at a party where they drank too much and...Gwen didn't like to think about it, but Deanna lost her virginity to Ian McCormick. She could have let it destroy their friendship, but Deanna felt terribly about it and she swore she'd never been more than just a friend with Ian and that's all it would ever be.

"Still," Deanna said. "I honestly didn't think you'd still be thinking of him at all."

How could she not? When they were kids, he'd actually been nice to her. He even talked to her and the conversations they had were real. Not about stupid stuff where she had to pretend to be interested in whatever football team was going to the playoffs or who got drunk at whatever party. But real stuff like what they hoped to achieve with their lives, what the future looked like and where they wanted to go to college. And besides that, he'd been so gorgeous. Correction, he *was* gorgeous. Maybe even more so, if that was possible.

But he still doesn't know you're alive, Gwen, the little voice in her head reminded her. She wasn't more than a townie friend back then, and she was even less now.

"So, he didn't recognize you?" Deanna changed tack. "Not that I'm surprised. You look like a totally different person. Seriously, if I didn't know better, I wouldn't even recognize you and we've been friends since…well, forever. You look crazy good."

Gwen blushed and waved away the compliment. She couldn't seem to get used to the attention she got from people who knew her *when*. It was almost easier for people to think she was just naturally thin and fit. Except when it came to her blog. But talking about her experiences online was a totally different thing. It was safe to hide behind the screen.

In fact, throughout her transformation, it had been a sort of therapy almost. Her website was the place she went to decompress and work through all the feelings that went along with her journey.

She should blog about Ian. Why hadn't she thought of that earlier? It made perfect sense. She could have a chance to process her feelings about seeing him again. *And still being invisible.* And she'd already made her summer vacation into an *event*. When she'd announced her plans to return to Cedar Springs, her readers had gone wild. They wrote in, offering suggestions as to how she should present her transformed self to her old friends, what she should do for a part-time job, and pretty much everything in between. It never ceased to amaze her how invested her readers were in her life and her weight loss journey. In fact, the whole *returning home* thing had garnered so much attention that a talent agent, Jade Johnson, had contacted Gwen about representation, a book deal, and a possible television deal. It was all too crazy to comprehend, but Gwen wasn't about to say no.

She swallowed the rest of her water quickly. "The next one needs alcohol."

"Really?"

Gwen nodded. "Yes. There are only sixty-four calories in vodka. And I'll just run a few extra miles tomorrow. It'll be worth it."

Deanna laughed. "Sounds good. Well, not the running part. I'll leave that up to you. But I don't have any patients tomorrow, so I'll have a few drinks to toast your return. I'll get Marcus to meet us at the Grizzly Paw when he's done up at the hill. He'll want to meet you. I have trouble remembering that you never knew him."

"Nope." Gwen shook her head. "He moved here after my last summer. But it sounds like a good plan to me." Gwen leaned down to retrieve her laptop from the bag at her feet. "But first I need to post an entry."

"Seriously? You just got here."

"I know." She smiled and tried not to take offense to her friend's expression. Ever since her blog started to get real attention and had actually started to make her money, most people had the same reaction. She'd definitely discovered that people struggled with the idea that you could actually make a living writing about your life. Hell, when the advertising offers had first started coming in, Gwen had trouble believing anyone would actually want to give her money to tell her story. "But it pays the bills, Dee. So as long as people want to read it, I'm going to write it."

She flipped open her laptop, signed onto Deanna's Wi-Fi and logged into her account before her fingers froze over the keys. "What do you think?" she asked her friend. "How should I write about Ian?"

"Ian?" Deanna shook her head. "You can't. I mean, you can't use his name or anything."

"Oh my God. Of course not! I don't use anyone's real name. I don't even say what town I'm in. That part is all anonymous. It has to be. But part of the success of everything is how real it all is. So…"

"You're going to blog about Ian?"

Gwen nodded. There really wasn't a question about it. In fact, she'd already kind of alluded to him in past posts as one of her catalysts for starting her weight loss journey. There was no doubt in her mind that if she'd been thin all those years ago, Ian would never have stood her up at the Summer Equinox festival. Not a chance.

"Wait." Deanna got that look in her eye that meant she'd just figured out the connection. "You've already blogged about him, haven't you?"

"You read my blog?"

Deanna gave her a look. "Of course I do. Since the beginning. And that's when you mentioned…Ian is Mr. Summer. How did I not see that until right now?"

Gwen laughed. "I have no idea. It's not like my feelings for him were a big secret or anything. Doesn't everyone remember my public humiliation?"

Deanna grabbed her hand and squeezed. "Gwen, no one remembers that. I promise."

"I remember."

Her friend laughed a little and moved away. "You're the only one. It wasn't even a big deal. He just didn't show up. It's not important. Let it go."

But as Deanna moved about the kitchen, cleaning up dishes and leaving Gwen to write her blog post, all she could think of was that it *was* important and there was no way she could let it go.

Dear Reader,

Sometimes things don't turn out quite the way you plan…

If you're anything like me, you've spent some time thinking about and maybe even daydreaming about how certain people from your past will react to seeing the new and healthier version of you after wronging you. Not to say that I've spent a lot of time thinking on this, but I'd be lying if I said I never thought of it. Of course, as I was planning my return to the town I'd spent all my summers, there was one person in particular that came to mind. Mr. Summer. Long-time readers will remember me mentioning Mr. Summer before. Every young woman—particularly those of us who've struggled with our body image…who hasn't—has at least one encounter with a boy or man that has stuck with them. An encounter for better or worse that somehow shaped or defined how they thought of members of the opposite sex, and sadly, how they thought of themselves.

That was Mr. Summer. I was desperately in love with him from the summers of fourteen to eighteen. Four years of my life in which he barely knew I was alive. When he finally did notice me, he humiliated me and broke my heart.

For years, he was the star of my fantasies when I thought about returning with my new and improved self. How would he react? Would his jaw drop? Would he stumble over his words as he apologized for standing me up all those years ago? Would he beg me to give me another chance?

Well, readers, I can tell you that now, all these years later I finally have my answer.

None of those things happened. In fact, he didn't even recognize me.

We came eye to eye and there wasn't even a flicker of acknowledgment in his eyes. (Which are still as dreamy as I remember.)

And now I'm here, on the eve of my first night back in town and already I'm filled with a strong sense of dissatisfaction in regards to Mr. Summer. So, obviously I cannot let a homecoming come and go without doing something about it. Or can I?

What do you think? Should I confront Mr. Summer and thank him for being at least one of the catalysts that spurred my life change? Or should I let it go and move on? Or maybe something different....

Will Gwen let Ian know that they've met? Or will she play a game with him? And if she does...who will win?
Find out NOW! Read Love in the Moment for FREE!

About the Author

Elena Aitken is a USA Today Bestselling Author of more than forty romance and women's fiction novels. Living a stone's throw from the Rocky Mountains with her teenager twins, their two cats and a goofy rescue dog, Elena escapes into the mountains whenever life allows. She can often be found with her toes in the lake and a glass of wine in her hand, dreaming up her next book and working on her own happily ever after with her very own mountain man.

To learn more about Elena:
www.elenaaitken.com
elena@elenaaitken.com